The Vigilante Vixen and the Boston Bad Man

By

T. G. Partain

Happy Reading!
T. G. Partain

Chapter One

Snowflakes as big as butterflies landed against Pearl Hawthorne's cheeks and caught in her eyelashes. Swirling in the wind, the snow formed eerie patterns that looked like cold ghosts of wranglers and rustlers' past. Pearl hunched forward over her horse, Belle, soaking up her warmth. Belle snorted, blowing hot blasts of steam which quickly formed into ice crystals and blew back against them. Carefully they meandered through the steep mountain path toward the fork of Green River heading for Brown's Hole. From there Pearl knew it would be miles before she would be near enough to Brown's Hole to catch up with Rita.

Rustlin' Rita had made off with most of her pa's herd. It was a sight too late in the day to worry about how Rita had stolen the cattle. Her pa was all the family Pearl had in the world and those cattle were his livelihood. Even though she had been asleep when Rita and her ruthless brothers had raided the ranch, as far as her pa was concerned, Pearl was to blame for the theft of the herd. Back in the day, Pearl and Rita had both been wild as March hares and best chums, and no matter how much Pearl proclaimed her hatred for Rita now, her father figured they were still in cahoots. If she had been the son he had always wanted, instead of a "worthless female," none of this misfortune would have befallen him. In his mind, every bad thing that had ever happened to him was Pearl's fault, and the loss of his cattle was just the icing on his birthday cake. Pearl had to get them back. She had not thought twice about whether or not it was wise to follow a band of cutthroat cattle rustlers out into the howling winds of an approaching storm. She had packed her saddlebags, loaded her guns, and lit out after Rita's thieving bunch like there was no tomorrow. And for Pearl there was none. If she did not get those cattle back, her pa would never forgive her, and she could not live with that hanging over her for the rest of her days.

Besides, she wanted Rita to get her just desserts. Rita also had a hundred-dollar bounty on her head for other unlawful indiscretions, and Pearl saw the money as an added bonus. Pearl figured that dead or alive a cattle-stealing, backstabbing, soiled dove like Rita deserved to die. Rustlin' Rita was a "pistol-packing mama," but she figured she could handle her. Pearl wasn't exactly a "curds n' whey" gal herself.

The blowing snow held Pearl and Belle captive between the river and the cliff wall. Leaving the trail would spell their death, so Pearl fought like all tarnation to keep their keel. Deer had walked that same track since before she was born, so she knew better than to strike out on her own. Belle stumbled forward into yet another flurry. The wind was blowing harder, threatening to pitch them backward. Belle stopped, leaning against the solid surface of rock beside them.

"You can do it, ole gal," Pearl whispered. "Come on. Just a bit farther."

Belle trudged a couple of steps, whinnying sharply as another icy gust slammed into them. Pearl leaned over to stroke the horse's neck and wipe clear her face. Belle sneezed hard and staggered back. The wind picked up, blasting them against the rock.

Pearl coaxed the horse forward anyway. They could not stay where they were. The river screamed through its traces like a heathen demon racing through the cold. Belle cried out, echoing their tormentor, and Pearl kicked her right flank. Hard.

"Move." Belle held tight. "Move, damn it." Pearl held her knees tightly against Belle's side and urged the animal forward.

A break in the wind coupled with the insistent rocking of Pearl's body against Belle's back encouraged her to plod ahead. As they inched along, she prayed that Belle could feel the trail beneath them, but Pearl feared greatly that she could not. The horse's hoofs skittered and clacked against the stony pathway. The ground was covered with snow, making it hard to see where to go. Faint traces of bare earth could be seen amongst a trio of trees off to their right. She headed the horse toward them, hoping against hope they could have a moment's respite from the storm.

As though the bay could read her thoughts, Belle surged onward. Slipping and sliding into the small grove of trees, Belle struggled to maintain her balance. The dark patches of earth Pearl had mistaken for dry ground were really covered with ice. Damn. The horse fought hard to stay standing. Finally, she slammed into a Shagbark Juniper, and Pearl grabbed onto it holding them fast against the blowing snow.

"We're okay. Good ole, Belle. You done right by us." Gripping the rough arm of a branch, Pearl enfolded them into the scaly green leaves. Pungent and sharp, the aroma of the tree and its fruit comforted them. They needed the brace, and the tree limbs held them as the wind continued to gust around them.

Blizzards were killers, sure and certain, and Pearl had no intention of dying or of letting Belle perish, either. Nothing had ever stopped her in life. Abandoned by a shiftless mother shortly after she was born and stuck with the moniker of Pearl Hawthorne by Sister Mary Naomi at the orphanage where she was taken, she had stubbornly made her way. The good sister, an avid reader of Hawthorne and Melville, had decided that Pearl needed a name to remind the child of her sinful start in life, hence the name Pearl from the book *The Scarlet Letter* and the addition of Hawthorne its creator. Years later, Pearl's real father had seen the error of his ways and had come forth to claim her when she was eleven. She had remained a Hawthorne. She liked Hawthorne better than her pa's name—Pecker. Pearl Pecker. Eleven years old was old enough to know that anyone named Pearl Pecker was going to catch hell for the rest of her natural-born life.

The sister had said Pearl was a product of lust and sin, and she was never allowed to forget it. So later, after reaching her womanhood, she had dabbled in both—and had found out the hard way that even though sin was a good time for a short time; it would make life the devil in the long run. Still, she was a robust good-looking woman and had enjoyed the lustful moments, and now, captured by an icy desperado of a blizzard, she remembered one or two of her distant paramours. There was nothing like a frost-bitten horse and a Shagbark tree to make a woman long for a strong embrace and a warm bed.

Pearl yawned. The thought of a warm quilt covering her frozen limbs was intoxicating. She closed her eyes and leaned over the saddle horn. Belle, too, was cold, so Pearl snuggled as much against her as she could. She felt so tired. Her eyes were heavy; she did not want to stay awake any longer. Pearl longed for the escape of sleep.

Freezing and murderous in its intensity, the wind crashed them against the rough, peeling bark of the Juniper. As they hit the tree, dozens of slender branches covered with prickly leaves scratched stinging welts across Pearl's face. She jerked awake. A close call. Sleeping meant death. She should not go to sleep. The branches whipped against her again. Pearl swatted a scaly cluster away from her face and snatched some of the hard, blue berries from its center. She crammed the berries into her mouth, biting through their tough skins into the bitter sharp center.

The taste brought tears to her eyes, but it also woke her up. She gagged but still ate a few more. Even though she had some provisions in her saddlebags, she needed the acrid inducement to keep her alert. Her bandana was wrapped tightly around her neck, so she pulled it free to cover her face. Immediately, the cold hit her neck and with it a shiver that racked her body. Hurriedly, she pulled the collar of her jacket up around her neck. Her wind-chapped cheeks felt warmer without the harsh sting of the storm against them.

Again, Pearl bent forward over the horse and ran her hands across the bay's face. It was coated with snow; ice crystals had formed on Belle's long lashes and around her nostrils. Belle moved her head from side to side trying to soak up her mistress's touch. A sudden inspiration had Pearl rummaging through her bag for her bonnet. She slipped from the saddle and slid around the horse. Looking eye to eye with her old friend, Pearl said, "You probably ain't going to like this, but it's the best I can do under the circumstances."

She unfurled the bonnet and tied it around the horse's neck. The bravolet was a good thirteen or fourteen inches long, so it went way down the horse's neck and around the sides of her face. Pearl mashed the wide brim together and then yanked it down to help shelter Belle's face. Thank goodness she usually preferred a sunbonnet; a poke bonnet wouldn't have been worth a tinker's damn. The larger bonnet provided enough cover to protect the mare's face but still allowed her to see ahead.

"Now ain't you pretty?" she said. "I hope this works, girl."

Pearl remounted and urged the horse away from the shelter of the trees and back on what she hope was the trail. She decided that she would stay between the cliff and the water for as long as she could. At some point though, she and Belle might have to cross the river. Hoping like all hell for a miracle, the frozen pair struggled from the trees and were soon back on the trail.

Just shy a mile of traveling, Pearl realized the track was growing wider and less easy to read. She kept between the cliff wall and the river and tried to maintain her place on the deer trail. Keeping to a set path wasn't just important; it could mean life or death. Here trees grew more profusely and acted as a buttress against the wind. For a brief time, Pearl and Belle could relax, not have to fight so hard.

Letting down their guards, though, proved to be a mistake. For as soon as they took a deep breath, the blizzard let go with all her might. Pearl screamed as the snow whipped through the open canyon. Her cry was lost in the blinding barrage as she and Belle were swept tumbling backward, off the trail, end to end, toward the raging river.

Chapter Two

Cut into the bank was a godown for horses to be able to enter the river to cross. On the opposite bank was its twin. Unfortunately, the trail split at the point where Pearl and Belle had stopped. The wind tossed Pearl off the path and into some scrub. Belle had been shoved onto the descent leading to the godown. The mare's shrill scream was lost in the wind, but Pearl knew instinctively which way her four-legged partner had fallen.

Grabbing hold to some scraggly brush, Pearl pulled herself upright and surveyed the trail. A spot of blood shone brightly on the new fallen snow. Pearl patted her arms and legs and touched her face. She did not seem to be hurt. That could only mean one thing. Belle was injured. The thought made Pearl's heart race. No matter what happened, she would try her damnedest to save Belle. Pearl righted and cinched her weather-beaten old hat. Her hair had come loose from its pins and shone like ebony fingers against the pallor of her skin. She did her best to tuck it back under the hat, but it was a lost cause.

The horse whinnied again, and this time Pearl heard it. Shuffling across the powdery ground, she grabbed first one bush and then another until she came to the start of the godown. Her heart stopped beating when she saw Belle lying on her side, her back legs in the edge of the frothing river. With every move, the horse slid an inch or two into the water.

"Belle. Stop." Pearl screamed and slid down on her haunches to see the situation better. "This is bad, ole gal. Just be still. I'm a coming on down." She tried to quiet her voice, but it shook with fear and anger. Anger at herself for going after that no-good bitch, Rita, and then anger at Rita for stealing what was not hers in the first place.

As she scooted on her bottom down the godown, she muttered and cussed Rita for all she was worth. "That no account lily-livered whore is going to see how high the cat jumps when I get a hold to her. Taking what ain't hern to take, is going to cost her plenty. Why, I'm a mind to string her up and then ask questions." Then to the horse, "you just stay still, baby girl. I'll get you out of this mess if it's the last thing I do and takes the last breath I got in me."

Pearl hope that Belle's back legs stayed strong and didn't go numb in the freezing water. If the horse could not pull herself up, she was lost. Pearl stopped near a cottonwood and caught her breath. There were several trees close to the riverbank. With a sigh, she untied her long waterproof outer skirt and pulled it loose at the waist. She yanked it down over the men's trousers she always wore under it. Even though she usually wore outer skirts, she found trousers more practical for riding and working. She slung the skirt over a tree limb and eased her way down to the horse.

Luckily, the saddlebags and her rifle had not yet reached the water. After she stroked Belle's face, she pulled the gun free, shoved it away from the water up the bank, and then worked to untie the bags. She couldn't pry them loose. Her fingers were too clumsy in her gloves, so she pulled one hand free to work the string. Her fingers clenched in the cold. She yanked hard on the string and felt it slide. As she prized it loose, the horse slid a little farther into the water.

Belle's eyes rolled in terror. She started to thrash, causing her body to continue to slip. White foam appeared around her lips, and Pearl prayed the horse hadn't punctured a lung. She pulled the bridle from under Belle's head, thankful it hadn't snagged on a rock.

She patted Belle's face and leaned close. "Don't move," she whispered. "I'll save you. I promise." She pulled the crazy-colored sunbonnet over Belle's eyes, and the horse quieted down.

Pearl snatched the lariat from her saddle and reached under the side of the horse checking the cinch. Hers was a center-fire rig, so the cinch was in the middle of Belle's belly. She didn't want to tie onto the saddle only to have it pull free. The cinch was tight. Looping a larks head over the saddle horn, she pulled. Pearl smiled grimly, remembering her pa teaching her to tie knots. She had tried hard to prove her worth to him. No matter how proficient a hand she had become, nothing she did ever satisfied him. Getting his cattle back meant everything to her. She wanted—no, she needed his approval.

Pearl stood and pulled her glove back on. Then she surveyed the situation and decided things couldn't look much grimmer. Belle was in serious danger. She could freeze to death or be swept away. The godown was slippery. She gathered the rope and dug her boots into the trail. Crunching and cussing her way to the trees, she worked to straighten the rope and find a place to tie off. When she reached the nearest scrub, she wrapped the rope around it and tried to wench the sodden animal from its watery trap. On the first yank, the horse didn't budge. The second tug gave Belle the encouragement she needed to try and regain her footing.

The horse raised her head and planted her front hooves into the icy bank. With nary a sound, the scrub pulled free of its mooring and the horse started to pitch back, but she held her ground. The rope slid out of Pearl's hands.

"Stay put, Belle." Pearl scrambled to catch the rope and tie it to a larger tree. "Damn, damn, damn. Come here, you mangy scrap of hemp." She caught the rope and walked it around a cottonwood. Her fingers were numb with cold, so she slapped them together before she gritted her teeth and pulled with all her might. "Son of a preacher's biscuit eater," she cussed and pulled. Then she looked up at the heavens. "I sure ain't helping my case none. Am I, Lord? Sorry about that."

The taut rope burned through the leather of her gloves and creased her palms. She pulled her lips together tightly and concentrated for all she was worth. The rope whined against the tree, cutting into the bark.

Once it was tied, she called down to Belle, "Come on. Now, girl. Up with you."

The horse thrashed back and forth and finally stood. Belle's back legs shook a wobbly dance as she came up the side of the cut. Pearl never let up on the rope. She continued to walk the rope up the trail, until she was able to coax Belle into the stand of trees. Once the bay was safe, Pearl descended alongside her and grabbed a hold of the bridle.

She buried her face in Belle's straggly wet mane. "Dear Lord, thank you. I would've never thought we could do it."

Methodically, she began to pat down the horse and found a jagged cut in Belle's left shoulder. It was oozing blood, but by the look of it, the cut was superficial. Pearl pressed her fingers hard against the wound, applying strong pressure to stop the bleeding. She pulled a rag from her saddlebag and wiped the horse down as best she could. Her pants were wet from the knees down, there was nothing for it, and so she grabbed her skirt from where it hung on the tree branches and yanked it up around her waist. It was a heavy article of female attire, but it helped alleviate her chills.

Pearl hadn't noticed the blizzard's master had reined in his storm like a cowboy breaking a bucking bronc. A deadly quiet fell over the day. The sky started to darken. The gloaming created shadows in the trees and made it hard to find the way back to the deer trail, but Pearl surged forward to the cliff wall, guiding Belled behind her. Hours had passed, since the blizzard had unseated her. She had to keep going. She had to find shelter.

As she regained the trail, she noticed the faint whisper of a smell. So slight in the evening breeze, she thought she was imagining it. She saw a floating whirl of smoke drifting lazily through the sky above the cliff wall. Smoke. Someone, somewhere, had built a fire. At that moment, she didn't care much if the fire belonged to friend or foe. She would handle the situation when she got there. She just wanted to feel a lick of warmth in her hands and in her feet.

Pearl swung back into the saddle and rode slowly down the trail. Maybe, she had ridden farther that day than she had thought. The only shelter that she knew of in the canyon was Warren's cabin, a prospector's cabin that had been abandoned. To get there, she had to follow the deer trail up the canyon wall on the east side and then pass through a gap at the top of the wall. When they got up the trail, though, it was tricky at the top.

Dismounting, she sidled along a narrow ledge to the gap. Once Pearl and Belle passed through the gap, though, she could make out the cabin down below them. It was a low split-log building with a wind break shelter attached to its side. Smoke was boiling from the open doorway.

"What the hell?"

With a shout, Pearl leapt into the saddle, slapped the mare on the rump, and rushed down the slight hill to the cabin. As she drew near, she could hear a horse whinnying from the wind break. Its hooves beat against the wall as it struggled to get free. Belle halted, bucking slightly backward.

"Come on, girl."

Belle was having none of it. Pearl figured, and rightly so, that the bay had had her share of excitement for one day. Pearl jumped down from the horse.

Just then, a man came hurtling from the open door. Flailing and coughing, he fell into the snow. His horse, having broken free from its hitch, raced out of the side shelter and took off into the night. The man crawled toward Pearl digging his way through the snow. She couldn't help but notice how handsome he was, still she and Bell took a step back. She didn't need any more complications. Another storm was building, and Rustlin' Rita was out there somewhere with her pa's cattle.

"Help! Help me." The stranger collapsed right at Pearl's feet.

"Hells bells. Why me?" she asked, but no one answered.

Chapter Three

Pearl stood stock-still, looking first at the smoking cabin and then at the man. She had a mind to let him lay there and die. The dern damn fool had probably set the cabin on fire, and it was the only shelter for miles. Normally, she would have ridden on until she had gotten closer to Brown's Hole, but the weather was an unpredictable bitch that night, and she didn't want to chance her luck any more for the day. Besides, she and Belle both needed to sit a spell and rest. Some supper wouldn't hurt her feelings none either.

It was quite a dilemma. Save the man first or try and save the cabin. She could hear the voices of her childhood, those blasted, blessed nuns, telling her to do the right thing. Pearl's idea of rightness wasn't exactly the same as the holy sisters had been. Still, she bent over and rolled the stranger onto his back.

He was breathing—a little raggedy, but he was breathing. Smoke stains ringed his nostrils and soot covered his cheeks. He was out cold. Holding his face by the jaw, she turned his head one way and then the other, looking closely at his face. She had never seen him before. He moaned, and she jumped to her feet.

"Watch him," she said to Belle. "If he wakes up, don't let him get away."

As though she understood every word, the mare leaned over the prostrate figure and watched his face. Unmoving, unblinking, the horse waited.

When Pearl reached the open doorway of the house, she realized the smoke hadn't dissipated. Fanning her arms about, she waved the smoke away from her face and pushed the planked door to one side. There was no fire. Instead, a heaping pile of Shagbark leaves and cones belched smoke from the open fireplace. They had been too damp to burn but not too wet to smoke. It took only a moment for Pearl to realize that the stranger hadn't checked the fireplace before he had tried to build a fire. She searched around the rugged stone hearth and found a yard-long sharpened stick leaning against the wall.

"Damned dogged idiot." She poked at the branches. She pulled her bandana up over her mouth and nose and bent to her knees. Ramming the stick up inside the flue, she was able to jab a piece of metal jammed up into the fireplace. The obstruction acted as a damper to keep the cold weather and varmints out of the flue. Poking the damper over and over with the stick, Pearl was finally able to dislodge it. With a creak and a slam, it fell open and the smoke was sucked up through the flue and into the night. Pearl cleared out the mess of leaves from the firebox and set about making a decent fire.

Outside in the yard, Luther Van Buren III began to stir. Belle nudged his face with her nose and moved closer waiting for him to awake. His eyelashes flickered and finally fluttered open. Luther caught his breath as the mare snorted against his face. Her breath was horrible. Startled, he reared back against the cold ground and found himself staring into Belle's huge, liquid brown eyes. She smiled, and her big yellow choppers were mere inches from his nose.

"Ashhh!" Luther began scooting backwards from the horse's face, but she steadfastly edged along with him. "Help! Help!" He flailed about in the snow trying to escape from the bonneted mare.

Pearl wondered what in the hell all the commotion was about. The fire finally caught, so she was loath to leave it until it was burning steadily. Twig by twig, she ripped apart the branches and fed them into the fire. As if it were a hungry child, the flame grabbed the brittle offerings and ate them up. Soon, she was able to add a few larger branches to it. Once the fire was hotter and had a few coals, she could begin to add a log or two.

"Somebody, help me." The man's cries finally galvanized Pearl into going back outside. She paused at the door, taking in the scene. The man was still flat on his back with Belle standing guard over him. They looked a ridiculous sight. The black-suited stranger pursued by the bonnet-wearing bay. Every time the man tried to rise, Belle gently pushed him back with her nose. He kept waving his arms and shouting, but the horse was not afraid. Instead, she seemed almost amused.

Pearl crunched through the snow and patted Belle. Together they looked down into his flushed red face. Pearl scratched her head, thinking the situation over. Should she let him up now or find out what he was up to in this part of the country? By the looks of him, he was a mite too citified to be headed for an outlaw handout like Brown's Hole. But Pearl knew that sometimes looks could be deceiving, so she figured he might be some new breed of owlhoot.

"Move this horse away from me."

Pearl rubbed her jaw still considering the situation. She looked at Belle and thought. He hadn't asked her to move the horse. No, he had told her to move it. Pearl thought he was kind of uppity. She didn't say anything.

"Are you going to move this creature or not?"

"Not," she said and turned and marched back to the cabin. She kicked at the heaps of snow along the base of the house looking for a stack of firewood. There were only a couple of pieces by the firebox. Usually travelers through these parts left a stick or two of wood for the next fellow. Nary a stick was piled along the front, so Pearl moved on around to the shelter. Stomping and shoving at the snow, she scraped against a small pile just inside the lean to.

Betwixt and between the rugged shelter and a gnarled old Juniper was a pile of logs. They were dry, protected by the shelter's overhanging roof. She kicked at the top log dislodging it from the pile, and then she scooped it and several others up into her arms and headed for the house.

"You think you might quit flirting with my horse long enough to get some of this wood into that cabin yonder," she called over her shoulder. She laughed to herself to see the stranger trying to charge up against Belle's insistent defense. She climbed across the threshold into the house.

"Move out of my way, mangy beast."

Just as Pearl came out of the cabin for more firewood, he swatted at Belle, eventually hitting her against the nose. The mare's great eyes rolled back, and she bared her teeth again, but this time she wasn't smiling. She shook her head back and forth; the bonnet flapped this way and that. Belle pulled back to see the man better and to ascertain which body part of bite first.

"You oughtn't done that, mister. That sure was stupid of you."

Pearl came flying off the stoop at a full run for the horse. "Don't do it, old girl. He ain't worth it. If you bite him, you might get sick with the typhoid or something. He ain't from here, you know."

"Bite me?" Luther took another look at Belle's gleaming ivories and started scooting and pitching backward through the snow.

Finally, Pearl was able to grab the horse and bring her head around, for the more was bent on taking a plug out of the fast-talking city man. She laughed a good one, when he took off for the shed.

"Come on, dearie. Let's go up here and check on my fire." Pearl pulled the horse behind her. "That damn fool is so dumb he didn't even know how to build a fire. Probably a good un that he didn't though. He might've burnt down the cabin." Laughing Pearl rubbed Belle's nose, and they went on in the cabin.

The fire was dying down, so she stirred the coals just a mite and put a couple of the smaller logs on it. She needed to bring in more wood, but the fire was so tantalizing. Its warmth was beguiling. She reached out to its heat. Immediately, she felt warm pulses against her fingers, and she sighed. Still, the flames would soon die down, if she didn't have more wood to feed the fire.

"Hello. I need past your horse." The man had a cultured, British accent.

Wondering where he was from, Pearl stomped back to the open doorway.

He had an armload of logs, yet she didn't move aside. Meanwhile, his horse had trotted back into the clearing. It was a nice horse, and even from twenty or so yards away, Pearl could tell the saddle was a good one. Tooled leather and silver conches down its sides gave the saddle a Spanish style.

"These are heavy, you know," he said.

"Really?" Pearl looked as though she couldn't care less, but slowly and deliberately she did move.

The stranger tried to ease around Belle. She pushed him back, and Pearl laughed. The horse shoved him again causing him to fall and lose half his load. She was moving in to stomp him, when Pearl grabbed her reins and pulled her back.

"That is enough, Belle." Nose high, she walked past him, tugging Belle out the door and toward the lean to. "Why don't you take that wood into the house?" she asked. As he moved around her, Pearl had a sudden thought. "Just don't mess with the fire none. You ain't exactly a woodsman. Are you?"

He stared at Pearl and Belle.

"Well, now that that's out of the way, why don't you go on into the cabin, while I put up the horses?"

Clicking her tongue to call the other horse to her, Pearl went right over to the shelter to bed down Belle for the night. She pulled the saddle from her horse, and in a sudden fit of kindness, she did the same for the stranger's horse. The saddle blankets, especially Belle's, were damp, so she hung them over a section of railing to dry out. There was a slight pile of dried sweet grass in one corner and a tiny patch of green grass left over from summer growing in the rear of the shed.

When they were all three under the low hanging roof, Pearl asked, "What did you think of him, Belle?" She didn't wait for an answer but answered Belle's unspoken opinion. "You think he's good looking? Belle, be serious. He can't even build a fire."

Pearl caught Belle's eye and saw that she was looking at the tall dark horse of the stranger.

"So, that's it? You fall for the first handsome horse on the trail?"

Belle nodded as though to say, "Damn right."

Chapter Four

As Pearl walked back to the cabin, she vowed to not follow in the hoof prints of her horse. That is—she didn't intend to show any untoward interest in the Brit. For all she knew, he could be a gambler or a conniving son of a bitch, looking for someone to take. Either way, she wouldn't trust him no matter what.

Stomping through the snow, Pearl worked herself into a frenzy of hate and distrust, so that by the time she reached the open doorway, she was so mad she wanted to shoot the wily varmint and be done with him. She patted her bosom, feeling the slight bulge of her .41 Derringer hidden inside a pocket sewn onto the outside of her merino vest. If that high-falutin' foreigner tried to connive on her, he would have another think a' coming. She dared a peek at the shimmy covering her vest. The ivory handle of the little pistol was barely visible through the muslin. Yes siree, she ought to just shoot him right then. Right then and there.

Luther Van Buren III bent over the fire letting the feeling come back into his frozen body. His fingers, especially, tingled with the relief from the heat. He stamped his feet up and down trying to thaw them out. When Pearl walked into the room, she thought he looked like a black hawk, flapping and prancing in front of the fireplace.

"Thank you for the fire," he said. He bowed low, pulling his hat off with a flourish and a grin. "You saved my life."

"So, stranger, what's a dandy fellow like you doing out in these parts, anyhow?" Pearl stood in the doorway with her feet spread wide and her hands on her hips. Her rifle was propped by the door jamb just to her right. The cabin was sparsely furnished with only a couple of three-legged stools, a rickety table that had seen better days, and the frame of a bedstead against the far wall.

The stranger looked nonplused by her answer. "I'm meeting someone at Brown's Hole." He drew himself up stiffly looking Pearl up and down.

Pearl narrowed her eyes and considered his answer. "I'll lay a wager you do...so are you a gambler or an outlaw?"

The man seemed offended by her question. "Neither, madam. I am Luther Van Buren the third, and I'm traveling to Brown's Hole to visit my fiancée's ranch. She is an extraordinary woman, and we plan to be married as soon as I arrive. And you are?"

Ignoring his question, yet intrigued by this information, Pearl closed the door behind her and walked closer to the fire. She loved a good tale as much as the next person, but she heard her stomach rumbling.

"You hungry?" She moved to her saddlebags and started pulling out some grub.

Luther watched her for a moment. "Actually, madam, I haven't eaten since this morning." He stepped aside to allow her access to the fireplace.

"Neither have I, so we're even there." She decided to brew up some coffee and heat up some salted bacon and a couple of biscuits. She had gotten a couple of boiled eggs that morning before leaving, and she figured she could share some grub for a good story. Besides, if the stranger turned out to be a swindler or a bad hombre, she could always shoot him.

She pulled a small tin pot out of her bag and handed it to Luther. "Make yourself useful and get some snow. I need some coffee."

She set about heating the rest of the food, and presently he returned with the pot of snow. Without a word, Pearl snatched it from his hand and thrust it onto the fireplace irons. The cold tin of the little pot hissed and popped as its moisture touched the hot grates, and the snow seemed to melt in an instant.

When the supper was cooked, she asked, "Well, where's your plate?" She held out her hand for it.

"I don't have a plate." Luther was flummoxed.

"Don't have a plate. Probably don't have a cup, either?"

"No."

"Cain't build a decent fire." Pearl shook her head. "Where the hell did you think you were going, Third Luther? Brown's Hole ain't exactly the big city. There ain't no hotels are nuthin' like that up there." She waved her hand around in a grand gesture indicating the interior of the cabin. "Does this look like Boston to you?"

"I am going to my dearly beloved's ranch, as I told you before. I'm sure it will be adequate for our needs."

Pearl recalled the various cabins and shacks in Brown's Hole. A ranch, though. Who up there owned a ranch? She shoveled some of the food onto her plate and handed it across. Then, she grabbed her spoon and started eating from the pan.

"May I have a fork?"

"Use your digits. I only got one spoon, and I'm using it."

She bent over the pot, eating and not talking. She poured a cup of coffee and savored its bitter heat. "I only got the one cup, too; but you're welcome to use it when I'm done."

Waving the spoon in his direction, she said, "Go on with your story. Who you know up at Brown's Hole with a ranch? What's your fiancée's name?" Pearl couldn't think of any women ranch owners.

Luther took a few bits of his food. The bread was dry and hard, and the bacon tasted extremely salty. Bits of biscuit stuck to the back of his tongue, making him cough and sputter.

"What kind of bread is this? It's horrible."

Well, excuse the hell out of me." Pearl looked down at her biscuit, then chewed thoughtfully. "They're soda biscuits. Miss Menken back at the hotel in Vernal made this up for me, but she was almost out of flour. They do taste a mite soda-ie"

"I'm sorry to sound ungrateful. It's just that they are so dry."

To his utter dismay, Pearl leaned over and poured her coffee on his plate. Coffee grounds swirled over the mashed-up biscuits and eggs. Almost immediately, the coffee was absorbed by the bread.

"Why I'll be damned. That bread was dry," said Pearl. "It soaked that coffee up just like an oriental sponge."

Luther just stared at his plate.

"Well, ain't you going to eat it?"

He set the plate to one side and looked at Pearl in silence. He smiled.

Something about his smile made her uncomfortable. She fidgeted back and forth on the rough edge of her three-legged stool. "You ought to eat that food, and that's good advice. Trust me; you'll be glad tomorrow that you got a meal." She considered him thoughtfully. "Lessen you brought some food with you..."

He picked up the plate and started to eat again.

Pearl wiped her nose with the back of her hand and took stock of her company. His hands looked smooth, no scratches or scars. No rough work. This was no wrangler—maybe he was a card man. His face was clean-shaven, which was a rare sight in the Utah Territory. The winters were so cold. He had a barber shop haircut, too.

"Well, go one with your story. Tell me more about this fiancée. Have you even met this woman?"

"I've decided to hold my counsel. I'm beginning to find your interest unseemly," he said.

"Oh, that ain't so." Pouring another cup of coffee, she smiled and nodded. "Humph. Unseemly." Taking a sip of her coffee, she considered his reply. "That's okay then. I don't think you got no sweetheart up in these parts." All of her former anger returned. "I think you must be some kind of outlaw or varmint." A new idea struck her. "Either that or a preacher, and I don't like them none better than pole cats."

"Now look here, madam. I think we've gotten off to a bad start." He stood as though to apologize, but Pearl saw his stance as a challenge.

Eyes blazing, mouth set in a thin straight line, she jumped to her feet facing him. "I should've left you to choke to death or freeze in the snow. "But, no," she contradicted herself, "I do the Christian thing, like any decent woman? And what do you do? You, you bastard, you belly ache about my cooking and then get all uppity and act like I ain't good enough to meet your bride to be."

"Meet Rita? I said nothing about you meeting Rita."

Pearl's eyes narrowed into tiny slits. She leaned forward, and all the while her right hand was reaching behind her for her Winchester.

"Who did you say?"

He faltered, but then stood straight and declared proudly, "Rita Odena Lay. The only woman ranch holder in Wyoming." Luther should have kept quiet after that. "She owns over a hundred head of cattle, and we are going to be married and live out our days on her ranch."

Pearl's fingers made contact with the Winchester and wrapped around the cold shaft of steel. With a high-pitched scream that sounded like a tea kettle about to pop its lid, she whipped the gun in front of her. Pointing it straight at Luther's nose, she said, "Rita. I'm going to give your darling Rita a little wedding present. I'm going to dress dear Rita in a hemp for-in-hand for the wedding. It'll be the last necklace she ever wears."

Chapter Five

The click of the Winchester's lever echoed in the room. Luther reached for the side arm strapped to his waist, but his hand was shaking so badly the gun slipped from his fingers to the floor. Pearl took a step forward, holding her rifle steady. A soft red cloud covered her vision. She was beyond anger—she wanted to kill.

"Mister, you move again, and I swear to God I'll blow your damn head smooth off your body." Pearl shook her head trying to clear her vision.

Rita. This sissified Englishman Redcoat, varmint was engaged to Rita. Her mind hissed and coiled like a diamond-back rattler waiting to strike. Russlin' Rita married and curled up in bed with Third Luther here. The very idea made her even madder. Not that she wanted Rita's man. Hell, she wouldn't have him if he came gift-wrapped with a new bow, but to think of that soiled dove Rita running her thieving, cattle-rustling paws all over Luther's six foot two, good-smelling body was just too much. She would shoot him, before she let Rita have him.

Then Luther asked a very stupid question. "Do you know my darling Rita?"

Pearl's mind whirled like a phantasm riding a whirlwind. She couldn't decide if Luther Van Buren III was the dumbest jack rabbit in the desert or if he was a wily coyote outlaw about to be married to his larcenous lady. Except that Rita was no lady. She was a livestock looting bitch, and Pearl wanted to track her sorry ass down and hang her. Hang her and then shoot her.

"No," she said, and her sarcasm was lost on Luther.

"Well if you don't know her, why are you so angry? You're about to shoot me, and we've never even been properly introduced."

Pearl's lessons on manners kicked back in. She propped the rifle against her right shoulder and put out her left hand. "Pearl Hawthorne." She shook his hand, noting as she did so, that it was a nice handshake—firm and not at all afraid.

"Your hand is as smooth as a baby's butt. Haven't you ever done any hard work? I felt girls' hands that were harder than yours," Pearl said.

"I'll have you know, Miss Hawthorne, I am a dentist. In fact, I have just been admiring your teeth." He pointed at her mouth. "Why, when you bare them like that, I can see that you've been most diligent in caring for your dentures."

"Dentures! I ain't wearing dentures. These are my own teeth." She aimed her gun at him once again.

"Of course, they are. I was referring to your teeth. All dentists use the correct terminology for teeth—dentures."

"This is all very tea party talk, but let's get back to your wedding story. Maybe I don't know this Rita." She lowered the gun a couple of inches. "Tell me more about her."

Listening to Luther had started Pearl thinking. What if he didn't know Rita's cattle were really Pearl's pa's? Could he innocently lead her straight to Rita and *her* cattle? Pearl decided to play dumb. "Maybe we did start our jig on the wrong foot," she said.

"I would feel much better if you put that dreadful gun away," Luther said.

"Well, hell, I'll just bet you would." After she lowered the lever, she placed the rifle back against the door jamb.

Eyeing one another warily, they both sat back down by the fire. Luther began to regale Pearl with tidbits from his letters from Rita—tales about her cattle, anecdote about one of her dogs. Pearl followed every note and nuance of his story. She kept silent throughout the tale. Thinking. It was clear this idiot Luther was in love with Rita—but with a Rita he had yet to meet.

"Let me get this straight. You two haven't ever met—in person. You're a mail-order groom. Like a mail-order bride...only different? You ain't bad looking. How much did you cost, if I may ask?

"Cost!?" Luther jumped to his feet again.

Pearl leapt up as well, grabbing her rifle as she did. "You better settle on down, now. I ain't putting up with no hollering. I jest asked you a simple question. It ain't like I asked if you were a virgin or nothing. You ain't a virgin, are you?"

His face bright red, Luther stuttered and sputtered as he tried to regain control of his composure. "Madam, you are severely trying my patience."

"That's a shame," she said. "You're kind of pissing me off, too, but you don't see me getting all persnickety about it none. Matter of fact, I think I've handled this whole situation like a perfect lady."

He snorted.

Pearl cocked the lever on the Winchester.

Taking a deep breath, Luther smiled. Pearl smiled back but retained her grip on the rifle. Cautiously, Luther began to lower himself onto his stool. Pearl did the same. Neither blinked as they stared straight into the other's eyes. The game had grown as deadly as a Mexican standoff. The only difference was that Pearl held the gun, and she was not afraid to use it. In fact, with each passing second, she longed to shoot Luther Van Buren III, male, mail-order groom, even more. Moments of silence ticked by as Pearl weighed the benefits and deficits of shooting Luther.

Then, her thoughts flashed back to her pa's face the morning he faced the terrible facts. Rita and her brothers had stolen his herd—lock, stock, and barrel. He had looked over the empty pasture, and then he had looked at Pearl. She could tell by the look in his eyes that he blamed her. She had stood there, her bare feet wet with the early morning dew, absorbing his hate and his disappointment.

"Pa... I'll find who did this and get them back for you."

"You can't do nothing," he had said. "You're just a scrawny girl. If you had been a boy, then maybe now I'd have a man to help me. But you? You go back in the house and get yourself dressed and get to work."

All of Pearl's years of back breaking work taking care of his cattle and his house had boiled down to nothing. To her pa, she was nothing but the sum of her female parts. Then and there, she had vowed to find the cattle rustling varmint that had taken their herd and bring them back to her pa. Maybe then, he would see her what she was—a woman—a woman that was as strong and capable as any son could be.

"Pearl," Luther said and waved his hand in front of her face. "Pearl, I'm sorry."

With his apology, Luther had won her attention. "I'm sorry. I shouldn't have don't that. You not only saved my life; you fed me. You're exactly right. You have behaved most perfectly as a lady."

Pearl nodded and balanced her gun back against the door post. "Damn straight. Now, let's go to bed."

"What?" Luther's gaze roamed about the room, finding only a solitary bed frame.

Advancing until she was right under his nose, Pearl gave Luther's face the utmost scrutiny. "Get you mind out of the boudoir, Third Luther. It's time to get some sleep. Tomorrow will be here before we know it; and I, for one, need some shut-eye."

"Of course." He laughed, relieved. "I'll check on the horses and bring in my saddlebag." Cautiously, he edged around her and pulled open the door.

Clouds of snow blew belligerently in through the doorway coating them. Pearl shoved Luther all the way through the door and slammed it shut behind him. Then she set about making a pallet for herself by the fire. Gladly, she would give the bed to Luther. For all she knew, it was choc full of bugs. Still, it was cold, so maybe it only housed a couple of mice. Either way, her bedroll would do her fine.

A couple of good-sized rocks were stacked alongside the fireplace. With a grunt, she heaved two of the stones into the fire to warm. After sweeping the dirt and ash away from the fireplace, she kicked the stools out of her way and unrolled her bedroll. Her heavy outer skirt, she shook out and lay on top of the pallet. The rocks had begun to faintly glow and were easily rolled out of the fire with the stick she had used to move the damper. With one hand, she held open her covers, and with the other she scooped the rocks into the bottom of the pallet. Warm feet meant a good night's sleep.

As Pearl was crawling into her bedroll, Luther burst into the room stomping the snow from his boots. His face looked raw from exposure to the freezing air. He slapped at his arms to gain some warmth. When his feet were clean enough, he crept closer to the fire.

"Your bed is over yonder," she said and pointed at the coarse and jagged wooden bed frame. With a sigh, she pulled her covers over her arms and lay back against the pallet. "And could you move away from me? You're dripping all over my pallet."

He hesitated, looking down at Pearl's hair spread across her shoulders. He was shocked
to find that she looked young and vulnerable. He had not seen her as anything but tough until
that moment. Under his gaze, a blush spread across the porcelain landscape of her face staining
her cheeks and causing her lips to bloom.

"You're very beautiful," he said. Unable to contain himself, Luther knelt down beside
her. "You are as lovely as a new English rose come into flower." Looking intently into her eyes,
he said, "I can't believe it."

Pearl's fingers clenched the rolled edge of her blanket. Part of her was mesmerized by his
dark brown eyes, and the other part of her was horrified. *Rustlin' Rita's fiancé wants me. He's
trying to seduce me.* Silently, she slipped a hand under the covers until she felt the bird's eye
handle of her tiny Derringer hidden in her wool vest next to her breast. Its handle felt smooth and
warm. Slowly and carefully, she pulled it free and held it under the covers. For just a moment,
the thought of bedding down with Luther seduced her. Men like Luther, sophisticated men, had
never been a part of Pearl's world, so she wasn't sure how to handle Luther's compliments. She
decided to shoot him.

"Believe this, you frisky fiancé," she said and pointed the revolver at the juncture
between his eyes. "I'll blow a hole right in the middle of your cheating forehead." She waved
toward his bed with her gun. "Now, get up real slow and move your double-crossing derriere
over to that bed, or I'll make Rita a widow fore she's even hitched."

Trying to salvage his pride and his neck all in one, Luther stumbled as he sought to
recover his balance and stand up. He tripped, falling hard against Pearl's leg and tumbling over.
His head connected with one of the rocks hidden under her covers. Right before he passed out,

he said, "You're warm. How are you so warm?" His vision swam, and he had a blurry vision of

Pearl right before she jumped up and kicked him off the pallet.

"I'm hot-blooded. That's why," she said.

Chapter Six

Around midnight, Luther woke up. He was lying on the floor, chilled to the bone and harboring a severe headache. He stood up and rambled dizzily around for a few minutes trying to figure out where he was and why it was so cold. Finally, he realized the fire had almost gone out, so he stirred the slumbering coals until a tiny flame burst through the ash. Using all the timber beside the rocky hearth, he managed to rekindle the fire until he could get it going hot enough to add a log and then much later, a couple of more.

Luther knelt in front of the fire savoring its warmth and listening to the steady growls of Pearl's snores. His fingers were stiff with cold, and the growing heat caused them to stretch wide as though to capture every bit of warmth they could. With a sigh, he looked back over his shoulder at the maiden martinet sleeping behind him. She was certainly tough enough for the West. Without a doubt, he knew that she was a stronger person than he was. For the first time, he wondered if his sweetheart was as fierce as this woman.

His fiancée, Miss Rita Odena Lay, had written the most exciting letters. Letters depicting the West as untamed and wild, letters that had made him long for a different life than his boring round of patients with their crusty molars and malodorous breaths. Sure, there were some days he enjoyed being a dentist, but more often than not he yearned for something more. Adventure. Passion. Years ago, he had left England, his motherland, to pursue a new future, to take on a new identity, and to escape the clutches of a pending betrothal.

Luther hadn't wanted circumstances and heredity to dictate his life. Without looking back, he had left on a ship heading for Boston. But life in Boston had turned out to be much like life in London. He had the same occupation, and he met the same kind of women. Then he had answered an advertisement in the newspaper—rich, ranch-holder seeking husband. At the time, it had seemed like such a lark; but now, in this cabin with a mountain woman stretched out on the floor behind him, he felt elation. He had done it.

If Rita Lay was anything like Pearl Hawthorne, he was in for a challenge. There was no doubt in his mind, though, that he could rise to the occasion and tame this wildcat. He threw back his shoulders and swaggered about in front of the fire. Yes, indeed, he was man enough for this woman and for Rita. With a smirk, he bowed before the sleeping beauty on the floor.

"Madam, Luther Van Buren III at your service." He turned and headed for the rickety bed frame propped against the wall. Nailed to the bedposts were crudely cut planks meant to support the straw and leaf-filled mattress.

Silently, Pearl snuck up behind him. As Luther bent over the bed, she raised her leg and kicked him solidly in the rear. Floundering around, trying to catch his balance, Luther keeled over onto the make-shift cot. For a second, it seemed as though the bed would hold his weight, but with a loud crack it broke in two. The heaviest piece of the structure, the headboard, wobbled for a second, settled, and then fell onto Luther's back.

Pearl dusted her hands off and said, "Looks like this ain't your night. Sir."

That was it for Luther. Resigned to his fate and his throbbing back, he rolled the headboard out of the way and pummeled the stick-filled mattress. Then he turned on his back and closed his eyes.

"Good night, Pearl."

Pearl was sorely disappointed. Fighting with Luther filled her with adrenalin. To have him back out of a ruckus so easily was disappointing. Still it was not quite light out yet, so she crawled back under the covers for another hour or so of sleep.

* * * *

Just as the first ray of light shone through the chink in the planked door, Pearl was up and out of her bedroll. The fire had almost burnt out again, and she had noticed that Luther was still asleep. After poking the fire, she added another small log to the fireplace. Last night's meal had taken most of her grub, so she decided to scout out the nearest creek bed. There had to be one fairly close by. It just made sense that travelers or past settlers would build a cabin close to a source of water and food.

From her saddlebag, Pearl grabbed three notched sticks and a piece of cord. A deadfall trap should work, if she could find a large flat rock to prop up. She rooted around the fireplace looking for a piece of food to bait a trap with. Nothing. Just as she was about to give up, she spied a goodly bit of egg yolk from their supper the night before stuck to the leg of one of the stools. Using her knife, she scraped off the egg and stuck it inside her vest.

As she was about to leave, she gathered up her long skirt and tied it around her waist. While sometimes a nuisance, the thick fabric of the skirt blocked the wind from her legs and even worked as an added shield from brambles and branches as she rode through the woods.

Pearl caught her breath as she stepped away from the cabin. The blizzard had ended during the night leaving the forest swept with snow. Before her, the colors of the rising sun painted reflections against the perfect canvas of earth and trees. Glistens of color and sparkles of light turned the morning into a brilliant kaleidoscope with Pearl at its center. She walked into the middle of the clearing, turning round and round with her arms outstretched as though to capture Mother Sun's essence and then fling it back out in joy.

The rumble of her stomach brought her back to reality. She laughed and patted her belly. Then, she listened for another sound—the sound of a nearby creek or river. Not hearing anything, she shrugged and began to retrace her journey from the previous night. Climbing uphill in the snow was an arduous task, and she was full of fire and vigor by the time she reached the trail to the ridge. Just before she started her climb, she heard the faint whisper of water running. It sounded like a small stream, but Pearl knew the hush of snow could silence almost anything.

Just as she suspected, the creek was almost covered over by snow. She stood back from the bank, looking for early morning signs of deer or rabbit. A few feet away, the faint tracks of a rabbit dotted the other side of the creek. She wandered down stream about ten yards or so where the creek narrowed and jumped over the water to the other side. Then, she backtracked up the side, slipping and grabbing at bushes and trees near the bank to keep from sliding into the icy waters.

Finally, she moved closer to the creek bed and set her trap. A large flat rock was easy work to pull from the muddy side of the bank. She tied a cord around the lower end of one of the sticks and then again around a catch stick. She put one end of the bait stick up against the rock and the other against the catch stick. Carefully, she placed the bit of egg yolk on the bait stick.

Pearl moved off a few yards from the water's edge and built a tiny fire. Using a rotten shagbark branch as a torch, she went back to the trap. Taking a huge gulp of air, she blew out the torch and waved the smoke around the trap to mask her scent.

When she was done, she left the creek and headed back for the ridge. Time was mostly what she needed now. Time for the rabbit to come back to the water for a quick sip and time to check out the trail past the ridge. If the deer trail was blocked, she and city-boy had their work cut out for them. Pearl figured she could handle it, but Third Luther was another story altogether.

Chapter Seven

Luther could hear Pearl whooping and hollering; and as he struggled to come awake, he wondered what all the fuss was about. He crawled over the cracked post of the bed. Bent over and hobbling, he made his way to the fireplace. A good fire was crackling in the hearth. He was struggling to stand up straight, when Pearl burst through the door waving a rabbit's carcass.

"We'll have supper tonight, Third Luther." She held up the rabbit. Its ears flopped down around its head. "It looks a mite old for my taste; still beggars can't be choosers." She admired her kill. "Didn't take more than an hour to catch this here critter, and I skinned it quicker than a whore gets hot in a church-house."

"Madam, would you please stop waving that creature around. You're spewing blood all over everything. Besides, there is no way I am partaking of that *hare* for my dinner."

"Well, Third Luther, that's just fine by me. I didn't know you had a saddlebag full of grub, or I'd have let you cook the supper last night."

Pearl could tell by the look on Luther's face that he didn't have any food.

"Just one question though, Mr. Dentures..."

"It's dentist. I am a dentist."

"Oh," she said and covered her mouth as though embarrassed, "my mistake. Mr. Denteest, didn't it occur to you to pack some supplies? Brown's Trail is a far piece away from Denver; and as I've said before, this ain't Boston or London with hotels and fancy restaurants all along the way."

Luther studied the tips of his hand-tooled boots. "As a matter of fact, I did consider bringing some food and supplies for Rita, but she had written me that the mountain trail was clear and easily traversable."

"When did you get that letter?"

"Just a couple of weeks ago, and I immediately came west to join my bride. There were adequate outposts along the way."

Grinning from ear to ear, Pearl stuck her tongue against the inside of her cheek to keep from bursting into laughter. "I see. And when was this here letter writ?"

Luther strolled over to his saddle bag and brought forth the letter with a flourish. His expression soon changed, becoming mottled. "Two months ago," he said.

"Yep, that's what I thought. Two months ago, these trails were clear and there weren't no blizzard a coming." Pearl looked and felt smug. "But now there are, and you should've had the good sense to bring you some food. So, if you want to turn up your fancy nose at my rabbit, that's okay by me. More for me to eat."

Pearl flung the rabbit on the table and tied its front legs together with the cord she had used with the trap. She gathered her bedroll and slung her saddlebags over her shoulder. Without looking back to see if Luther was following, she headed into the shed to saddle up Belle and collect her gear for the rest of the journey.

Her earlier joy at killing the rabbit dampened, Pearl decided that Third Luther could get to his fiancée on his own. That pole cat could starve to death for all she cared. She and Belle would ride on ahead and watch out for him over the canyon. The ridge of the canyon would steadily incline to another couple of thousand feet. Once at the top, she could easily see Luther if he met up with Rita. Because the rocky walls were almost straight up and down, they made the canyon easy for anyone on top to either guard their position or to ambush unwary visitors.

Pearl wasn't overly concerned about Rita waiting to ambush her. As far as Pearl knew, Rita didn't even suspect she was being followed. If Pearl hadn't overheard one of Rita's no-account, whiskey-slugging twin brothers bragging about making off with her pa's cattle and taking them to Brown's Hole one night while she was eating supper at the Vernal Hotel, she wouldn't have guessed that her old schoolmate was the cattle rustler. Rita had always tried to one up Pearl, but to steal her pa's cattle was taking things too far. The very next day, she had gone to the Sheriff and demanded to be sworn in as a bona fide vigilante.

One good shot was all Pearl figured she needed. She wasn't worried about Rita's brothers. They were as dumb as rocks; and without Rita to tell them what for and how far, those two didn't stand a chance against Pearl's Winchester. They would probably light out like two jack rabbits once she started pumping lead, anyway.

The mare seemed eager to be on the move again. Pearl wondered if Belle was as sick of Third Luther's horse, as she was of the man. The stallion called to Belle as Pearl led her out of the shed, but the mare didn't seem to hear.

"Had all you wanted of him? Huh, girl?" Pearl rubbed her horse's face. "We need to get off from these two. A man who don't even appreciate a good rabbit...hell, a man like that can just go hungry."

"I didn't mean to sound ungrateful..." Luther began.

"Yes, but you did." Pearl said over her shoulder. "So that's that. Have a good wedding and kiss the bride for me."

With that, Pearl saddled up and rode away from the cabin. And from Luther.

She didn't look back to see the disappointed scowl on Luther's face. Nor did she hear the heart-sick whinny of his horse. Belle heard it, but she followed the example of her mistress and plodded on through the snow, until they reached the deer trail, and then with a whoop and a gallop the pair disappeared from sight.

Once the deer trail turned into Brown's Trail for sure, the walls of the canyon rose straight up, rugged and dangerous. High above the edge of the cliff, eagles soared in ever encroaching concentric rings, almost like buzzards they stalked the lone rider and his stallion.

If Luther had known exactly where he was going, he probably wouldn't have felt so adventurous or excited about his destination—Brown's Hole. Notorious for its outlaw population, the Hole was also an uninviting end for such an arduous journey. Yes, he had escaped the blizzard. He had found shelter at the cabin and food for his horse, but it was difficult to overlook that without Pearl's help, he would have either frozen to death in the storm or burnt the cabin to the ground just by trying to light a simple fire.

Even now, he wasn't quite sure what had antagonized that woman the most. Just because he had no desire to eat rabbit and didn't intend to cultivate a taste for it was no reason to take off and leave a man stranded. Deep down, though, Luther suspected there was more to it than that. Perhaps, he should have tried to woo her. But Luther was an honorable man—most of the time— and the fact remained he *was* an engaged man. A man about to make the ultimate commitment to one of the most exciting women of the Wild West—Rita Odena Lay.

Luther pulled the worn sepia postcard from his pocket. The photograph was of a young, beautiful woman—ripe and in the bloom of life. Her long light hair, he supposed it was blond, fell around her shoulders and down her back. She was in partial profile, yet he could see the line of her face, the curve of her cheek, and a dimple near her smile. Her eyes looked compassionate. The swell of her breast was promising compared to her tiny waist and nicely rounded hips. This was a woman whose letters had captured not only his imagination but his heart.

Too bad, the woman in the photograph was not really Rita Odena Lay. Instead, she was Darling Dottie O'Donnell, a singer and actress from the Silver City Saloon in Colorado and Rita's third cousin once removed. Rita's profile did not lend itself to portraiture.

Carefully, Luther followed Belle's tracks until he came to a narrow passing by the creek. The prints disappeared. There was not a track or a trace of Belle or of Pearl on the other side. He climbed down from his horse and walked back and forth looking at the snow. It was as though horse and rider had disappeared. The creek was swollen with melting snow, so water had sloshed away most of the snow near the opposite bank. But even Luther was smart enough to know that some tracks should be visible across the way.

He looked down the creek bed and then up the other way, wondering as he did, if Pearl had ridden her horse through the rushing, freezing water.

He had no idea that Pearl was right above him, watching him from her vantage point on top of a rocky crag. She had urged Belle into the icy waters, up the creek to an obscure fork in the trail that led around the side of the canyon to the overhanging cliff above.

Luther Van Buren III had a passel of trouble awaiting him. If Pearl didn't shoot him or the eagles didn't swoop down and get him, then he was in for a heap of a jaw-dropping surprise when he met his fiancée. Luther had even a more immediate problem at hand, because balancing on the brushy arm of a juniper branch, just over his back, was a powerful, tawny cougar ready to pounce at any minute.

Chapter Eight

Rocky crevices provided the only hold for Pearl as she lay on her belly and pulled her prone body to the edge of the cliff. Her fingernails splintered off from trying to dig into the baked clay surface, and her shoulders ached with the effort of holding herself safe and still at the cliff's precipice. She had crawled out too far. Small chunks of clay began to break away from the edge, sending a shower of dust down into the creek below. Pearl held her breath, hoping against hope that Luther didn't look up. She certainly did not want him to know she was following him; but more than that, she didn't need him to see her in peril.

Below her, Luther was trying to figure out which way to go, but Pearl figured that being lost was the least of his problems. If Luther confronted that mountain lion, and if the cougar smelled his fear, then Luther Van Buren III was history. Pearl's outer skirt felt like it weighed one hundred pounds; plus, it had ridden up over her knees and higher. The front of her thighs and her knees stung from their scratches and from burns made from scooting along the clay shelf. It didn't help that the ledge was bathed in glaring, bright sunlight.

Inch by excruciating inch, she pushed back away from the edge. If she could get her foot braced against a nearby stunted Pinyon, she could let go of the rocky rim and slide back a bit. Then, she stood a chance of saving Luther's life. Wildly, her foot groped behind her for support. She found none. Pearl's shoulders burned from exertion. She closed her eyes and let go of the crevice, expecting to slide down the rock face and even fall off the back of the narrow ledge. Instead, she only slid about an inch. She moved her foot back and forth, hoping that soon her boot would collide with something solid. The tip of her boot struck a rock. In her desperation, Pearl imagined she had bumped the side of the tree behind her. Actually, the pine was almost a foot to the right of the rock.

Even though she was in one hell of a predicament, Pearl was still a whole lot safer than the man below. With every move he made, the cougar adjusted his position on the tree limb. Pearl decided that the only thing saving Third Luther was his complete and total stupidity. She could not see how a grown man could be totally oblivious to an almost two-hundred-pound cat behind him. Didn't he have any natural instincts?

"Hell fire, I ought to leave the dumb ass to that cat. He stands a better chance of getting away from a mountain lion than he does Rita Odena." She snorted. "It's a sight prettier than she is, too." She looked at Luther's horse. "And that jackass ain't no help a'tall."

Luther's horse didn't seem much smarter than his owner, but at least he had moseyed across the creek and was standing on the other side. Pearl knew that she would kick Belle's butt, if she ever failed to warn her of another approaching animal—cat or cub. But the stallion had noticed a clump of grass poking through the snow and headed for it.

That mountain lion was one mean ole son of a gun who hated men and white men in particular. He wasn't hungry so much as he was ornery. His golden eyes gleamed with malice. He hunkered down, ready to spring.

Pearl saw that gleam and pushed back against the rock face with all her might. With a whoosh, she slid down the rock and passed the tree. Her heart felt like it was in her throat, but she raked her nails against the rock, clawing for all she was worth. Finally, she was able to grab onto a shrub growing from the side of the trail. She snagged it and held on tightly. Grunting and cussing, she pulled herself to her feet, turned around, and sliding and slipping down the rock trail, she careened into Belle. In one swift move, Pearl yanked her Winchester from her saddle.

She heard Luther's painful cry mingled with the cougar's howl of triumph. Sheer blinding anger coursed through her veins. Pearl turned and retraced the way she had come, back up the narrow cliff face. Swaying and scraping against the rock, she made it to the tree. She came around the front of it and braced her back against it, working the lever of her rifle.

Fire flew from the muzzle as she cracked one shot after another at the mountain lion. The large, powerful body of the cougar covered Luther's body. As far as she could tell, the cat had jumped onto Luther's back. Her first shot went wild, but the second grazed the cougar's tailbone. A strip of fur flew from his backside. The feline twisted in a hissing frenzy of agony. Pearl worked the lever a third time, but the old cougar had learned his lesson. He leaped off Luther's back at a dead run for the trail.

Frozen in his tracks, the stallion watched in horror as the mountain lion headed straight at him, but that varmint wasn't interested in man or beast at that particular moment. He wanted to get the hell out of there, before Pearl's Winchester sawed off another hunk of his hide. Luther's horse leapt out of the cat's way, and the cougar lit out another. He was headed for home. The cougar might have hated the white man, that was for sure, but he was damned if he would mess with one of their females. In one glance, he had seen the look in Pearl's eyes, and it was a sight he would never forget. Besides, he had a chip out of his tail bone to remind him lessen he ever decided to mess with a woman's man again.

Pearl didn't waste any time coming down from the ridge. She scampered right down to Belle, swung her leg up and over the horse. "Get on, ole gal. We've got to save our man."

Pearl saw that cross-eyed look of Belle's. "Okay, her man." The concession embarrassed Pearl. "He's too pretty to let the cat eat him up." She kept on grumbling. "He ain't got a chance with that she-cat Rita, either. If he's still alive and kicking, I could always kidnap him and use him for ransom. That's one way to get them cattle back."

When Pearl reached the creek, she rode up beside the dark horse and grabbed his reins. She didn't trust the horse not to take off, so she tied him to Belle's saddle horn. Then she looked over to where Luther lay face down by the creek bed. The back of his jacket had a tear right down the middle, but it didn't appear to be bloody, which Pearl took as a good sign.

With no regard for anything but Luther, Pearl knelt down on the muddy bank of the creek and touched the back of his head. She slid her hand down the length of his back, feeling for a breath, finding the broad expanse of his shoulders. Nothing.

Frightened, she reached both hands under his arm and pulled him over. She sat down fully on the ground and pulled him into her lap. Water soaked through the bottom of her skirt, but she didn't have a mind for that.

Luther's face was pale, whiter than anyone's she had ever seen. A jagged cut where he had hit his head on a rock showed starkly against his pallor. Carefully, tenderly, she traced the outline of the cut. She cradled his head against her chest. Unusual feelings broke forth inside Pearl, feelings she didn't know how to deal with.

Luther's lips turned a dark blue. He was not breathing. With a start, Pearl pushed him off her lap onto his back. Her head against his chest, Pearl listened for a heartbeat. She could not hear anything for the rushing of the creek and the pounding of her heart. She titled his head back and forced open his mouth, feeling inside for his tongue. Her fingers made contact with it and then pulled his mouth open wider.

As her lips touched his icy cold ones, Pearl could not help but think that their first kiss was probably his last. With her left hand, she pinched his nose and started to pump her breath into his body. Unconsciously, she prayed. With each breath, she thought *let him live.* She worked, until she was exhausted. Finally, he coughed. It was just a tiny cough, barely a whisper. But Pearl heard it.

She grabbed Luther's jacket and pulled him to her for a real kiss, but great bursts of chocking cough broke against her face. Luther struggled to regain his breath. His head flopped back, and instinctively he reached for something solid to hold on to. He grabbed Pearl's breast, trying to hang on for dear life.

Suddenly, Pearl was furious. She had just saved this varmint's life, and he was grabbing for her womanhood. Oh no, he wasn't! She threw Luther back onto the ground. With a shout, she jumped to her feet and kicked him hard in the side, almost knocking the breath out of him again.

"What are you doing, woman?" he yelped.

"I was trying to save your worthless life, but you, you stinking polecat, took a hold of something that weren't yours to get."

"Well, I never," said Luther.

"That's right, mister. You ain't never—not now and not later. I didn't save you from getting mauled by that cougar to have you turn your paws on me. That's for dang sure."

Pearl stomped away from Luther. She was so mad she could have spit cactus needles. Why the nerve of that fickle fiancé!

"Pearl..." Luther tried to sit up and talk sensibly, but it was too late. Pearl sloshed through the creek to her horse. She untied the stallion and rode on down the trail.

The last Luther saw of Pearl she was rounding a bend in the trail, headed round the wall of the canyon. His horse was following right behind her.

About that time, the first snowflake of the day fell right into Luther's eye.

Chapter Nine

Pearl would have felt a lot worse about leaving Luther stranded by the creek, if she had known another blizzard was about to hit. Since she did not, though, she rode hell for leather for the next mile, until she was able to get some of her madness worn off. For some reason, Luther got under her skin. She knew there was no way she could want a citified dentist who was engaged to a cattle rustler. Especially since said rustler was none other than her arch nemesis Rustlin' Rita Odena Lay.

Pearl and Rita had hated each other for years and nothing or nobody was going to change that fact any time soon. Still, Pearl knew she needed to keep a level head on her shoulders. She was a sworn-in vigilante, and she had pledged to uphold the law and bring in any and all cattle rustlers in these parts. Dead or alive. As far as she was concerned, Rita didn't need any other judge or jury than Pearl herself. There wouldn't be a deliberation. Rita was guilty. Beat the gavel. Case closed.

The end of a rope would be Rita's courtroom. Pearl would spell out Rita's charges. She might, if she was in the mood, listen to Rita's defense, but the verdict was in, and it wasn't a good one. The very thought of seeing Rustlin' Rita swinging from a rope gave Pearl a smile. Yep, ole Rita would die of throat trouble, gurgling on a rope.

Luther. Hell, Luther was extra baggage. After a spell of riding, Pearl figured she could find her bounty without Third Luther. Once she got on Rita's trail, he would just be a pain in the ass, anyway. It wasn't as if he was going to be singing with his tail up when his fiancée got to choking.

Pearl had known Luther's horse was following close behind, but she hadn't given it much thought, until she noticed that Belle was slowing down, allowing the other horse to keep up with them. She reined the mare in and looked back over her shoulder at the stallion. He was keeping a good distance, but he still wasn't heading back to his master. If Belle ever deserted her like this hombre had ditched Luther, she would sell that traitor at the next town. Not that Luther had a chance in hell of catching up with them. She whirled Belle around and charged at the other horse.

"Shoo, now. Get on back to Luther, fore something bad happens to him. He could be et up by that wildcat by now."

The stallion stayed put. In disgust, Pearl watched as he sidled up to Belle and tried to nuzzle against her nose. Belle wasn't moving away.

"Damn, love birds." With a yank, she reined Belle's head back out of his way. "And you, you damn hussy. One night in a shed and you're a soiled dove hooked on the first stallion that comes in the barn."

The wind started to pick up, blowing snow from the branches overhead. Pearl looked at the sky. She realized she hadn't been paying attention to Mother Nature's signals. The temperature had dropped considerably, and the sky had turned dark gray. The sun was bravely trying to combat the encroaching gloom, but is was a hard fight, and the sun was losing.

All of a sudden, Pearl had a vision of Luther floundering in the storm. Her heart skipped a beat. Her imagination conjured up vision after vision of Luther wandering aimlessly like a tiny chick abandoned by its mother. Even though Pearl wanted to see Rustlin' Rita dancing her last jig on the end of a short rope, she could not bear the thought of Luther staggering to his death, lost and frostbitten in the blinding snow.

Her heels dug into Belle's side. "Hee-yah, let's move, ole gal. Luther's probably breathing his last as we stand around here twiddling our thumbs and you flirt with disaster. Any fool can tell that stallion's all wrong for you, but you just ain't a listening. Are you, Belle?"

Of course, Pearl was schooling herself as well as Belle, but nothing short of a miracle would ever get her to admit it. Pearl's upbringing had taught her to ignore her feelings and to focus on the needs of others. After she had finally escaped the orphanage, Pearl had given her love and attention to her pa and his ranch. She soon figured out though that as far as old man Pecker was concerned, Pear was a liability that he tolerated but never truly appreciated. And Luther? While she might not want to admit it, Pearl felt something for Luther. She shook her head. If nothing else, she felt responsible for him. She knew firsthand that he lacked the skills to survive in the West.

The horses and rider pushed back into the face of the storm. They were brave and hearty rescuers, heading to save a man who seemed defenseless against the coming tempest. Pearl leaned forward as far as she dared over her saddle horn, straining to see the trail. The pull of her body onward urged her horse to go harder, move faster.

Belle was sure-footed and brave. The mare squared her shoulders and led Pearl and the stallion into the coming fray. Pearl was counting on her, and the bay was able and strong.

* * * *

"Pearl! Pearl..." Luther rasped, his throat raw from screaming. "Pearl, I'm sorry." He stumbled over a rock on the trail, falling hard, twisting his wrist as he fell. "Arrgh." He turned onto his back, holding his wrist and feeling every painful bump and bruise.

"Pearl, help me. Pearl, come back," he called over and over.

Pearl, however, was still a mile away, and Luther had no way of knowing she was returning to rescue him. He still could not believe she had left him like that. Of course, she owed him nothing. But to take his horse, leaving him to walk the rest of the way to Brown's Hole was, to him, unconscionable. What had possessed her to do such a thing?

Luther started to shiver, and it felt like the tremors were raking through the very fabric of his skin. The shakes came again and again. His fingers felt numb. Trying to shelter his hands from the freezing wind, he pulled them up into his jacket sleeves. Even though he was wearing a heavy overcoat, the cold crept through stealing his breath. Again, and again, he stumbled and fell. Each time he had to force himself to stand.

His arms and legs began to feel leaden, so that he did not want to move them. When he thought he could continue no longer, he headed for a small alcove in the side of the cliff. A couple of feet of jutting rock provided a natural awning overhead. He learned into the opening and shut his eyes for just a moment. His breathing stilled, and he rested. After a few moments, Luther mustered up the energy to scan his surroundings.

Forty- and fifty-foot cottonwoods were interspersed with junipers and various forms of scrub and bushes. Clusters of trees jutted forth from rocky inclines, and clumps of yellow grass hung tightly to the side of boulders and burst forth from crevices along the stony path. Flurries of snow were beginning to whip and whirl around and through the trees. The temperature was dropping faster now. Luther could feel the chill invading his bones. He needed shelter— somewhere safe and warm to ride out the storm.

As though the gods were watching and had decided to be benevolent to him, the wind ceased to blow for five long minutes. During the lull, Luther was able to see something in the woods ahead of him. It was a shelter, and it looked as though it were only thirty more feet away.

With an effort, he pushed away from the face of the rock and flung himself forward, moving as fast as he could go before the storm returned. Instinctively, he knew the storm was coming back. Without a moment to lose, Luther stumbled ahead. At last he reached his destination.

Before him stood the most unlikely shelter. Wooden poles skinned of their bark rose twenty feet into the air. They were covered with dressed buffalo hides sewn tightly together with sinew. Across the face of the Indian lodge, for it looked to be of native design, were painted horizontal alternating stripes of yellow and brown. Above the stripes, three crosses adorned the opening to the lodge. Luther did not stop to consider the ramifications of entering an Indian lodge. He was freezing to death, and he needed to escape the coming storm.

He circled the tent, until he found the opening flap. Gratefully, he pushed the buffalo skin aside and entered the lodge. Once inside, Luther pulled the flap shut against the wind. Light and noise disappeared, swallowed up by the stillness. He moved cautiously into the dark, quiet center of the structure and lay down under a wooden stand set into the middle of the room. Animal skins covered the area under the wooden poles. He lay down on the furs, curled tightly into a ball, and went to sleep.

Silently and without leaving even the smallest of tracks, an old Blackfoot woman moved along the outside of the burial lodge of her granddaughter. Her fists clenched when she thought of the white man inside. Tonight, her granddaughter would have a gift to take with her to her heavenly home. The old woman may have embraced some of the teaching of the pretres, but she was still a Blackfoot, and she would take the white intruder's scalp and leave it with the body of her only grandchild.

Chapter Ten

As the snow continued to fall, Pearl pushed on, desperately trying to find Luther. She felt guilty, but she was angry, too. Damn that Luther for coming to wed that hillbilly harpy, Rita. If he had an ounce of common sense, he would have stayed in Boston where he belonged. Hell, if it were up to her, he would have his rear end on the first boat back to London. What was he thinking coming over to a land he didn't know and hitching up with the ugliest soiled dove in the West?

Pearl knew that Luther couldn't have met Rustlin' Rita because, according to local legend, Rita Odena Lay was the spittin' image of George Washington. While Rita's distant relative might have once been the President, he sure made an unattractive woman. Pearl was known to describe Rita as "bone ugly and not getting purty anytime soon."

After an hour of tough riding, Pearl found herself straining to see any sign of Luther. The blowing winds heaped drifts against any immovable object, and she looked carefully at every lump in the snow. Luther could have fallen, and if so, he would have been covered completely in minutes. One large mound captured her attention, but when she and Belle went to investigate, it was only a boulder.

Luther's horse followed their return trip closer than he had their departure. Not sure whether he wanted the safety of their company, or if he, too, wanted to find his master, Pearl made certain he was within reach. She did not want to find Luther only to lose his stallion.

Pearl stopped her horse and looked in every direction. The wind had died down for the moment, but soon it would start up again. She could feel the momentum of the storm growing. She felt as though a gigantic monster was gaining strength—readying itself to attack.

Where was Luther? She was not sure how far he could travel on foot. Her best guess was that he would have waited a while for her to return, and when she didn't, he would have come after her. She couldn't be of that. She did not know Luther well enough to gauge his reactions. Nor did she know his level of stamina. What if he had traveled farther than this point? As she looked frantically around at the white silhouettes of trees and rocks, she wondered if Luther were out there. Frozen. Dead.

Pearl urged the horses forward along the trail. She would go on a little longer, but she had to find shelter soon. She was obliged to shield the horses. Even though she was worried about Luther, she could not let the horses suffer for her mistake. She had ridden for hours. Belle and the stallion needed water. Traveling in such extreme weather required the utmost exertion, and the horses would soon become dehydrated. If they were too weak to move, Pearl would be in a heap of trouble. They could all die.

A feeling so strong it knocked the breath from her caused Pearl to double over against the saddle horn. She lay hunched over her horse for a moment. Yes, she felt the cold and the impending doom of the storm, but she felt something else. Someone was watching her. She closed her eyes, trying to get a bearing on the sensation. Slowly, she opened her eyes. Without moving her head, she let her gaze wander over the terrain. She looked down the outline of the canyon walls and noticed an indention in the snow. It looked packed down, as if someone had stood there for a while.

Without kicking up a fuss, Pearl nudged Belle toward the spot. Before she could get to the wall, the stallion reared up. Pearl grabbed for his reins, cursing herself for not taking them sooner. He bucked away from her. Belle swerved sideways, moving away from the thrashing stallion. Pearl saw his eyes roll back in terror. Something was fast approaching. She could hear it behind her. In seconds, she noticed Luther's footprints against the face of the cliff wall and realized they had been protected by the rocky overhang. Luther was missing and whatever or whoever was behind her was not the genteel Bostonian. She could smell her attacker approaching, and nothing could stop it now.

The horses reared and whinnied in their distress. What was behind her? Pearl pulled Belle's reins sharply to the left, trying to move her away from the face of the rock. Whatever was behind her had them trapped. Pearl thought of the old saying "trapped between a rock and a hard place" and knew it to be true. Out of the corner of her eye, she saw a creature, large and covered with fur, careening toward her. This creature was no animal. It was a person covered in bear hides and brandishing the sharpest hatchet Pearl had ever seen. The hatchet chopped through the air again and again—coming closer and closer to Pearl.

The eyes of the attacker were colder and more deadly than the fiercest blizzard. Pearl's heart raced—beating out its warning like a tom-tom declaring war. The attacker screamed, and Pearl could see every tooth in her head. Belle must have seen the attacker at the same time as Pearl; because instead of jumping away, Belle charged into the side of the person knocking her to the side. Pearl grabbed her Winchester by the barrel and swung it hard at her opponent. She missed. The Blackfoot woman, hurdled against a tree by Belle's defense, had fallen just out of Pearl's reach. Even though the old Blackfoot woman hit the tree hard, she scrambled to her feet and came at Pearl again.

Pearl slid off Belle and crouched low holding the riflelike a club. She was ready for this fandango. Swinging the gun back and forth, she danced to the right and then to the left.

"Grrrr. You don't know who you're fighting, Grandma," said Pearl through gritted teeth. She was surprised at her attacker's age and agility. The Blackfoot woman looked to be at least seventy years old.

The Indian ran toward Pearl, hurling the hatchet as she came closer. Pearl ducked to one side, swinging wildly. The barrel of the rifle was cold and slick. It slipped out of Pearl's hands sending the gun flying into the snow. The hatchet glanced off the rock face of the canyon wall. Pearl snatched it up intending to launch it back, but the old woman tackled her to the ground.

The packed ice felt like solid rock. Pearl slid backward as she struggled to get her attacker off her chest. The older woman was covered with bear skins, so grabbing her was difficult. Pearl's Winchester had been lost in the snow, but she still held on to the hatchet. She slammed with the handle of the hatchet, poking it into the older woman's back.

The Blackfoot woman's face looked like the weathered face of an eagle. Her nose curved beak-like, and she raked at Pearl with her talons trying to get at Pearl's neck. Her eyes were black as sin yet ringed white around the edges. A thin scar ran down her cheek, and Pearl recognized her as Ida Iron Woman. Fear, cold and hard, formed a knot in Pearl's chest. Ida Iron Woman was the most feared of the Blackfoot women. Pearl could feel the old woman's fingers reaching for her neck.

"You trying to choke me, Grandma?" Pearl gave the old woman a shove that sent her sprawling back into the snow. "Well it ain't going to happen, you old Injun. Not today, anyway."

With a shriek, Ida Iron Woman leapt onto Pearl again. The smell of Ida's fresh sweat mixed with the musky aroma of bear was suffocating for Pearl. This time Ida succeeded in getting her hands around Pearl's throat. Nothing could have prepared Pearl for the sensation of being choked. Her throat felt like it was on fire. As she gasped for breath, she began to see red.

She dropped the hatchet. She grabbed at Iron Woman's hands, but it was like grabbing onto hands of stone. There were unyielding, deadly. Pearl kicked and bucked.

Her mind whirled with possibilities of escape. She reached beside her groping for the rifle. Finally, her fingers closed on the barrel of the long gun. Inching it to her. Time felt like it had stopped. Ida Iron Woman squeezed with all her might. Her nails dug into the soft flesh of Pearl's neck.

At last, Pearl was able to get her hand around the barrel of the gun. With all her might, she heaved the rifle into the air and slammed it down on the side of Iron Woman's head. Blood spurted from the old Indian's ear. She screamed and fell back off of Pearl. Retching and writhing in the snow, she covered her head with her hands. Blood splattered the pure whiteness of the snow. Its coppery smell fouled the air.

Pearl's throat felt like it had been scrubbed out with a carpenter's rasp. Every breath hurt. She turned onto her hands and knees, crawling away from Ida Iron Woman. When she was able to stand, Pearl walked on rubbery legs to Belle. Belle stood stock still and let Pearl hang against her for a moment. Then, Pearl rummaged in the bag hanging from her saddle. She pulled out a silver flask of whiskey. As she unscrewed the lid, she leant back against the mare, watching Ida Iron Woman struggling in the snow.

There was no feeling in her eyes as Pearl studied the old woman trying to get her balance enough to stand. Her eardrum had ruptured when Pearl hit her with the gun. Just like a bird with a busted wing, Iron Woman flopped around trying to regain her equilibrium. Pearl felt no pity. She knew as sure as she stood there that the old woman would have choked her to death.

Pearl took a long drink of the whiskey. It burned a righteous path down her throat, causing her to cough and spit. "Damnation and hell fire in it. I know why they call this stuff tonsil varnish. It's just scoured the devil right out of me."

Ida Iron Woman smelt the rock gut singe of the whiskey and held her hand out for a drink. She gave Pearl the most pitiful look she had.

Pearl laughed and wiped her mouth. The Winchester was against her leg. She grabbed it and worked the lever, pointing it at Iron Woman's chest. She took another swig of the whiskey. Then she looked into the old woman's eyes.

"You look tuckered out, but I ain't fooled by your act. You'd kill me as soon as look at me, and I know that for a fact. But hell, I ain't never refused friend nor foe a drink of whiskey." She held out the flask.

Ida Iron Woman took a step forward, holding out her hand.

"Just one drink, though, cos I keep this for medicinal purposes."

Pearl pushed the flask into the old woman's gnarled hand. With nary a word, Iron Woman drank deeply, smacking her lips when she was done. She thrust the flask back into Pearl's hand.

"*Merci.*" Ida Iron Woman said.

Pearl nodded and pointed at Luther's tracks in the alcove.

"*Ou est l;homme?* Where is the man?"

Ida Iron Woman squinted her eyes and thought. Then she smiled showing the ragged gaps in her teeth. She fiddled around the hem of her bearskin coat and held up a scalp. She nodded as she watched Pearl's expression pale and then turn bright red.

The click of the Winchester's lever erased the old woman's toothy grin. She pointed into the woods. Just dimly, Pearl could see the outline of the burial lodge.

"*La'-bas.*" Iron Woman said.

Over there.

Now, Pearl understood the Blackfoot woman's rage. Luther had entered a sacred place. Rarely did a Blackfoot woman try to kill a white man. Pearl knew that the old woman would stop at nothing to protect her dead.

Pearl's heart stopped. If Luther was inside the lodge, he was probably dead, too. She looked at Ida Iron Woman. Then she leaned back against the horse and gave the matter some thought. The Winchester would have to be her means of getting the old woman to let her inside the lodge. With the barrel, she pointed in the direction of the lodge.

"*Non,*" said Iron Woman.

"Hell, yes," said Pearl. "Move it, grand-mere."

The lever of the Winchester clicked open and then slammed down. Ida Iron Woman shuffled off the edge of the trail toward the hut. The fur of her coat was matted with blood, and Pearl knew that her ear must hurt like the dickens. The old woman was a fighter, and Pearl admired her spunk.

When they got to the lodge, Ida Iron Woman turned and faced Pearl. She held the flap of the lodge tightly. The snowfall was increasing, and Pearl knew they needed to be inside the structure, but she also knew that nothing was going to induce the old woman to let her and the horses find shelter there.

Pearl nodded and stayed still. Her heart felt like a jack rabbit running from a wolf, but her eyes never shifted from those of the Indian. When Iron Woman went inside the lodge, Pearl found herself wondering who else might be inside. What if a whole herd of Blackfoot was hiding in there? Pearl knew she would be dead in seconds, and the next scalp hanging on old grandma's belt would be hers.

The flap of the lodge flew open. Old Iron Woman dragged Luther's body out of the lodge by his arms. She pulled him in front of Pearl and let him drop. Ida Iron Woman didn't look back as she reentered the burial lodge.

Pearl looked at Luther's unconscious face. "What am I going to do with you?" She looked into the tumultuous sky. Snow began to pelt down on them. Her arms spread wide, she demanded of the sky, "What am I going to do now?"

Chapter Eleven

The tent's opening flew wide and a long bony hand reached out and pointed deeper into the woods. Pearl peered into the dense forest ahead. The trail behind her was clear. Once they ventured into the underbrush, she would be lost. She wondered if it were the old Indian's plan to have them wander into the wilderness and die. On the other side of the fence, there was no place to shelter on the trail. Pearl had been over that path, and she knew it like the back of her hand.

Without a choice but to trust Ida, Pearl knelt and gently slapped Luther's cheek. He shuddered but did not come awake.

"Luther, can you hear me? Luther, please wake up."

Pearl touched his face. So many times in the past day, she had wanted to kill him. But she hadn't. Yes, Luther was a hapless idiot, but he wasn't bad. His face was smooth, unlined. He wasn't hard, instead Pearl realized that Luther was just unlucky—somehow always in the wrong place at the wrong time. She pulled at his hand. He didn't move.

Using everything she had, Pearl pushed her arms under Luther's back and up under his arms. Her face twisted in pain, as she pulled him up into a sitting position. He flopped over. She hoisted him up again and tried to pull him over to his horse.

"Come on, damn it. Wake up." She pulled and tugged on his jacket, trying her best to pick him up.

Pearl's antics had a witness. Ida Iron Woman was greatly amused to see Pearl struggling to get the man on his horse. A long-forgotten memory surfaced, and the old Indian woman laughed out loud. Many years ago, she, too, had been challenged by a man. She recognized Pearl's mixture of anger and lust. Oh yes, Ida Iron Woman understood the white woman, so she came out of the lodge and together they raised the man over the horse.

His arms dangled over the side of the horse, but he was on. Disgusted with herself for being so soft, Ida Iron Woman belied her name and led Pearl and Luther into the woods. Pearl grabbed Belle's bridle and trudged doggedly behind them. The trees moaned and creaked as they passed through them; their ghostly inhabitants warning Pearl away from the depths of the forest. Luther moaned and slightly moved. Finally, Ida Iron Woman stopped her shuffling parade at the side of Crow's Cavern, a warren of tunnels through the side of the canyon.

The set of Iron Woman's shoulders told Pearl that she was saving them. Reluctantly, but resolutely, the Indian woman showed Pearl the way into the caverns. As she turned to leave, Pearl tried to say, "*Merci,*" but Iron Woman raised her hand in farewell and left them. Silently, Pearl watched her hike back to the lodge.

Pearl turned back to survey the cavern. There was much to be done, and Third Luther was still in a terrible way. His hands glowed white in the murk of the cavern, and Pearl feared greatly that he had frostbite. She needed to get him warmed up, but she knew if she tried to warm his hands and feet first, she could inadvertently drive the cold blood toward his heart. The end result of her help could, in fact, be heart failure.

On their own, the horses moved deeper into the cavern. Any other time, Pearl would have found the curved striated walls interesting and beautiful, but she was filled with terror. What if this cavern housed all sorts of critters? Critters that might come back home at any minute. Her Winchester had served her well in the past, so she decided to let the devil get behind her with his scary whispers and concentrate on riding out his tantrums. The blizzard returned, and she was screaming in a full-out rant now. Pearl was thankful that Ida Iron Woman had seen fit to show her the cave. For without her help, Pearl, Third Luther, and the horses would be lost.

Luther's horse was keeping as close as possible to Belle; in the process, he was scraping Luther's head against the cave wall. Pearl grabbed his reins and pulled him away from the mare.

"Stop that fidgeting, you dern damn fool. You are going to knock Third Luther's head clean off, and then how's he going to think?" Pearl shook her head. Apparently, the horse was as senseless as his owner.

Without wasting another minute, Pearl found a good spot against the cavern wall to put her bedroll. She shook the blankets out on the ground, and then set about trying to get Luther off the back of his horse. Even though Pearl was a healthy woman with enough meat on her bones to last a day or two, taking Luther off that horse was still a chore.

"Come on, man." She pulled him from behind.

He didn't move.

She slapped him a good one on the ass and grabbed his jacket-tails with both hands and yanked again. His body moved an inch. Pearl moved around to look at the front of Luther. She shoved his arms back around to his sides and pushed his head up to look in his face. He was still dead to the world.

Holding his head up by the hair, she asked, "Luther, cain't you help me a'tall? You're about the most useless son of a biscuit eater I've ever seen. When we find Rita, I'm going to hand you over like a prize pig at the county fair."

By this time, Pearl was flustered and afraid. She didn't want Luther to die. Motherly instincts she never knew she possessed came flooding over her, and she moved back around to Luther's backside and pulled his jacket-tails with all her might. Whoosh and by-cracky, Luther slid off the side of his horse and landed in a clump right by the bedroll.

"Sorry about that, Third Luther. That fall was a fart-knocker for damn sure." She pushed and rolled him onto the bedroll. "If you was awake, that'd hurt like hell." Sudden inspiration made her smile. "See the good Lord does take care of babies and idiots."

Pearl swaddled Luther as best she could in the blankets and then set about taking care of the horses. Unbidden but not unwanted thoughts of her life in the orphanage came flooding back. She remembered trailing behind the sisters, as they worked in the kitchen and in the stables. She untied the saddles and hefted them from the backs of the horses, the smell of horse sweat and manure took her back in time. Once she had worked all afternoon with Sister Mary Paul mucking out the stalls and cleaning out their rickety wagon. She had asked the sister why there was not a man around to help them.

Sister Mary Paul had said, "Pearl, woman's work is never done, and besides no priest is going to dirty his hands raking out horse shit."

Pearl's laughter had pealed out, and she had repeated the last part to herself over and over, until Sister Mary Paul had grabbed her by the shoulders and reminded her that good little children could keep their mouths shut. Pearl had nodded. She loved a good secret as much as the next person, and it had delighted her greatly to figure out that Sister Mary Paul was human.

For more than a few minutes, Pearl had been trying to ignore the fact that she needed to get a fire going. Neither stick nor piece of scrub littered the floor of the cavern. To get the firewood they needed, Pearl would have to go back out into the blizzard. She shied away from the thought. Why couldn't she lay down with Luther and keep him warm? Didn't most women have it the other way around? The girls she knew would have had the big strong lover taking care of their needs.

Pearl snorted. What a good one! The cowpokes she knew were a smelly bunch who wouldn't be good company after a hard rain let alone a blizzard. She mustered up her courage and headed for the opening of the cave. The blizzard had whipped itself into a banshee frenzy, and the minute Pearl stepped out into the squall it knocked her back into the cave.

"What the hell am I doing?"

She pushed back out of the cave, but this time she grabbed hold of the rock face of the cavern wall and pulled herself along the side of the rock. Snow blew thick and hard, and Pearl couldn't see three feet in front of her. She was terrified to let go of the side of the cave entrance. She needed the solid rock to keep her bearings. She moved forward another ten steps from the opening of the cave.

Without warning, a sudden gust of wind picked her up like she was a toy boat on a turbulent sea of snow. The wind carried her away from the rocky fortress into a small grove of juniper. Pearl latched onto the first branch she could grab. With a crack, it snapped off in her hands. Hands shaking and praying with all her might, Pearl shoved the stick inside her coat and broke off another.

"How in the hell am I supposed to get back to the cave?" she yelled into the wind. Another gust threw her back into the branches. "Aw shucks, Pearl," she said to herself. "Stop trying to figure this out, and just get all the wood you can. This old storm will let up in a minute, and you'll be warm and toasty in that cave yonder."

Grit and gumption were all that kept Pearl alive that day. She stuffed branches and twigs and loose bark in all her pockets and inside the folds of her clothes. The waistband of her skirt was jammed with broken branches and their stiff fingers poked her in every place imaginable. Still, Pearl worked on. The idea of a warm fire, boiling water, and her rabbit stewing in her little pot spurred her to continue. Finally, Pearl figured she had stuck a stick in any and all available spots, so she held onto the tree and waited for a brief lull in the storm.

Her eyes burnt with the effort of trying to look for the cavern. Luckily, Pearl had a good sense of direction, and she soon was able to fix a course for the wall. Every footstep was an effort. The sticks and branches scratched at her skin, tearing ragged cuts into her arms. Her chest and stomach felt like a million ants were eating away her flesh. Pearl kept going.

Over and over she said, "Come on, Pearl honey. Not much further now. You can do it, Pearl. Don't be a baby. Stop crying. Just keep your head down and move!"

Shoulders hunched against the buffeting wind, Pearl could see the cave door. She sped up. Her heart started to sing with joy, and Pearl sang with it, "Glory, glory, hallelujah."

Arms pumping, legs pushing, she headed for the opening into the caverns. And then...there it was. The mangiest looking varmint she had ever seen—a scrawny yellow-eyed wolf. His coat was gray and raggedy, and he looked meaner than a rattlesnake. But there was one thing for sure and certain. At that moment, that wolf was not one bit meaner than Pearl. She was so mad; she was almost frothing at the bit. That cur was a rotten no good thief, for between his crusty old teeth was Pearl's rabbit.

"Oh no you don't," Pearl screamed. She launched herself forward throwing sticks right and left. "You ain't getting my supper. Hell, if'n you eat my rabbit, I'll kill you and cook your sorry ass for supper. Give me more to eat."

The wolf looked first one way and then the other. Pearl seemed to spread out in all directions. Rotten lengths of branches and limbs assailed his body, but he wasn't letting go of the rabbit. As he started to turn and run back into the cave, he could feel Pearl getting closer to his back. He turned and looked back in time to see her pull a gun from her bodice. Pearl had grabbed the tiny Derringer and was aiming at him.

A puff of smoke blew from the barrel and BAM! Pear hit his right ear, blowing off the tip. Still, he held to the rabbit. WHAM! She hit him again. This time she got his other ear. The wolf dropped the rabbit and ran like hell out of the cave.

Pissed and tired, Pearl walked over to see if the wolf had ruined her supper. She picked up the rabbit and brushed it off. Thankfully, it wasn't even chewed. Catching it up by the cord tied around its legs, she threw it onto her shoulder and started picking up her firewood.

Not much later, Pearl crept quietly into the center of the cave. Luther was still out like a light, the horses were bedded down together trying to stay warm, and Pearl settled into a heap on the floor. She was cold, hungry, and plumb tuckered out. One by one, she pulled the sticks out of her clothes and piled them together. They made a sorry little pile, but still when she had some of them in a tee-pee shaped stack, she struck a hell stick and lit the fire. The smell of sulfur from the match was comforting, and Pearl enjoyed its odor long after she blew it out.

She sat looking into the fire. There was still so much work to do, but she just couldn't do any more. She was so tired. She stood; and on wobbly legs, tottered over to Third Luther and fell down on the edge of the pallet. With a sigh, she pulled back the bedroll covers and climbed in beside him.

Luther felt solid but cold, so Pearl ran her hands up and down his body. Soon, he stirred and drew her close to his chest. She snuggled into him and slept.

Chapter Twelve

Around nightfall, Luther Van Buren III awoke. Every inch of his body ached, but he was alive. His last memory was hazy—he was in the storm and then he had gone inside a teepee or tent. An earthy smell, soft fur beneath his cheek, and deliverance from the wind. Just before he had gone to sleep, he remembered an intense feeling of gratitude.

What he did not remember was leaving that soft, maternal place. Even though night had fallen, light from the full moon filtered through the opening in the cavern. He could tell he was inside some cave or subterranean tunnel. He looked up at the ceiling, at its curves. The striations of clay, the creams, corals, oranges, and browns followed the bends and turns of the walls. Snores, loud snores, reverberated echoes from the horses. In the shadows, he could see his stallion bedded alongside Pearl's mare. And Pearl was curled warm and tight against him.

Luther touched her hair, and she sighed and snuggled closer to his chest. He realized that she had probably saved his life, yet again. Her body was warm, and he could feel that warmth soaking into his limbs, making him feel alive. She smelled like smoke and something else—something wild. He moved his hand down her back and encountered something slick and cold. She had hung the rabbit carcass over her shoulder and forgotten it. At first, Luther's fingers recoiled, but then he pulled the twine from her hand and laid the rabbit by their side.

As much as he hated to admit to himself, Luther relished the idea of something to eat. His stomach rumbled, and he knew they needed food to sustain them. Over Pearl's head, he could see the smoldering remains of a fire, and though he had not a clue as to how to cook a rabbit, he was certainly willing to give it a try. The more he thought about it, the more Luther was convinced he could cook.

Groaning, feeling every sore and miserable muscle, Luther eased out from under Pearl. As he stood, he wondered if Pearl had taken a stick and beaten him with it. Every part of him ached. On legs so stiff they felt like they were broken, he hobbled over to the fire. He stirred it. Only a few coals remained, so he added some sticks that Pearl had dropped onto it. It took, and a wary flame began to burn.

By the firelight, he could see bits of bark and twigs littered the cavern floor. He had no way of knowing that Pearl had staggered drunkenly around the fire, her coat shedding the collection of firewood around the cave like a snake shedding its skin. She had been so tired that she had not felt her loss. Luther wandered around the room, gathering the wood and slowly adding it to the fire. Within a few minutes, its warmth drew him forward to stand hands outstretched in front of it contemplating his new adventure.

Coming out West to marry Rita had caused him to meet Pearl. He glanced over his shoulder at her, sleeping soundly on the bedroll. He marveled with the idea that western women were so strong—so rugged. He compared his notion of Rita with Pearl, and he fervently hoped that his bride-to-be was half the woman Pearl was. He reached into his vest pocket and pulled out the picture Rita had sent him. To be sure, the fair-haired damsel on the postcard was a looker— delicate and fine-boned. Pearl had her share of womanly charms as well. His face reddened as he thought about those charms pressed tightly against him, warm and curvaceous.

Luther shook his head and pushed those unwanted thoughts from his mind. He was engaged to the lovely Rita; and to her, he must remain true. Still Pearl was the most capable and dependable woman he had ever met. Quick tempered, too. He smiled thinking that Pearl's bad humor was like lightening—you never knew when it was going to strike, and you sure didn't want it to hit you.

Never having cooked before, Luther thought back to the night before when Pearl had heated up some bacon and biscuits. He dug through Pearl's saddlebags and found one stuffed with a small bag of feed for the bay and the other with her cooking utensils. Luther decided a little pot would do for the rabbit. The rabbit was about a foot long stretched out from tip to toe. He untied the cord and slipped it from the rabbit's body. He looked the rabbit over, trying to decide how to cook it. Finally, he decided to stuff it inside the little pot. The rabbit was a mite too long for the pot. When he pushed the head in, the feet popped out. Carefully, he folded the feet under the rabbit's body. He set the pot directly into the fire.

Pearl's horse and Luther's stallion got to their feet and stomped about, trying to regain their balance. In front of each horse, Luther poured a small pile of the horse feed. He was reluctant to feed them everything in the bag, even though they could easily have eaten it all. He was afraid of what Pearl might say, if she found out that he had given them everything.

The rabbit started to sizzle in the pot, and at first the smell of meet cooking was wonderful and almost overwhelming. Soon, though, smoke began boiling from the pot, and even a novice like Luther could tell that something had gone horribly awry with his recipe. He reached for the handle of the little tin pot, but it was scorching hot and immediately burnt his fingers. The rabbit seemed to be burning faster, and more and more smoke billowed from the little pot. He wondered how such a small rabbit could produce such a large amount of fumes.

In desperation, Luther kicked the rabbit-filled pan off the fire. Pot and rabbit sailed through the air hitting the cavern wall. Wedged tightly and burnt to the bottom of the pan, the rabbit continued to smoke. Luther reached into the pan and yanked on a front leg, trying to extract the scorched carcass. The leg ripped clean off the body. He couldn't pick up the pan, and the rabbit was stuck tight to the bottom. Luther's mind was a complete blank. Then he remembered the spoon and frantically grabbed it from the saddlebag.

Jab after jab, he poked the smoking rabbit. Finally, he kicked the pan outside into the snow where it melted its way down to the ground. Once the pot was cooled, he peeled the rabbit out of it. The inside of the pot was a mess, and he used snow to clean it out as much as possible. So much for being a cook.

The snow stretched out in front of him, pristine clean, glittering in the moonlight. And a source of water. I'll boil the damn thing, he thought. So, he filled the pot with snow and took the stiff and blackened rabbit back into the cave to cook again.

When the snow melted, the horses moved closer to the fire. Belle boldly tried to take a nip from Luther's ear. Finally, he got the message that the horses were thirsty. There was no other container to hold water, so with great reluctance he let first one horse and then the other drink from the pot. In seconds, all the water was gone, so he went back into the snow and refilled the pot. This time, he allowed the water to come to a boil, and he put the rabbit back into the pot to cook.

The water was boiling, and the rabbit was smelling good. Pearl stretched out in the bedroll and opened her eyes. Like a hungry child, she leapt to her feet and headed for the fire.

Proudly, Luther strutted back and forth, smiling and looking for all the world like a great chef who had just mastered the most divine culinary treat. The rabbit would soon be done, and he imagined Pearl's delight.

Pearl looked in the pot. Then she looked at Luther. Finally, she could stand it no longer. She fumbled in the bodice of her vest and pulled out her Derringer. Pointing it in Luther's face, she asked, "What in the *h-e-double l* did you do to my rabbit?"

Chapter Thirteen

"I cooked it!"

The shriveled, overcooked little rabbit with its scorched meat and missing foot lay wedged in the tin pot. No longer was the pot shiny and silver, either. Instead, soot blackened the bottom and sides. Merely touching it caused the bearer's hands to be covered in sticky black paste.

Pearl peered into the broth in disbelief. Then she closed her eyes. Her chest started to heave. "That poor, damn bunny." She couldn't stop laughing. "You cooked it all right, Third Luther. I'd say you cooked the tarnation out of him. Son of a biscuit eater."

"Where's my plate?" Chuckles just kept coming. "Dear me. I ain't seen nothing like that..." She considered when if ever she'd had such an experience. "Hell, that's got to be a first. Yep, you ever get mad at your darling Rita, just cook her up some grub."

"It doesn't look that bad." Luther was truly offended. "I wanted to surprise you."

Pearl started laughing again. She bent over and held her sides as she tried to stop. "Well, you succeeded. I was as surprised as all get out. I was so surprised I almost wet my britches."

She covered her mouth and walked over to dig through the saddlebag for her plate and cup. Giggles hit her again. To think that Luther had cooked her supper. She needed to stop laughing and appreciate the effort, but then she thought about that miserable rabbit, and she started laughing all over again.

"Well, Luther, that was mighty nice of you." She tried to keep a straight face. "And I do appreciate it. Believe me I do. It's just that you ain't cut out to be a cook. If'n I was you, I'd stick to them dentures. I'm sure you're real good with them." She nodded at the rabbit. "Cooking takes a while. But you know, Luther, we ain't got all day for you to learn right now. Folks could starve to death around here."

She pouted some of the broth off the rabbit and headed the cup to him. "I know you're hungry. Hell, I'm starving, but we need to warm our stomachs up some, before we fill 'em up with that meat. Take a swig or two of that broth, and then pass me the cup."

Even though the rabbit had looked awful, it was still meat. The broth was oily and warm. Luther relished the first sip. Wrapping both hands around the cup, he let the warmth permeate his hands, just like the broth was heating his stomach. He could feel its tiny flames spreading through his body. He took another sip, drinking deeply.

"Okay, Luther. That's good. Pass it over." Not sure what she was expecting, for the rabbit was certainly not visibly appealing, Pearl was nevertheless surprised at how wonderful the broth tasted. Immediately, she felt her body succumb to its nourishment. She sighed and relaxed, as she took another sip.

In short order, they drank the rest of the broth, swapping the cup back and forth and refilling it before they began eating the rabbit. And though the rabbit was boiled hard, and the meat was stringy, they both agreed that it was the best rabbit they had ever eaten. Of course, for Luther, it was the only rabbit he had eaten, but he did not mention that fact, and Pearl was too polite to ask.

After the meal, Pearl made a spot of coffee, and they shared it in silence. Their journey had been fraught with so many trials—so many setbacks. Yet looking at Luther, Pearl inexplicably felt that they had come a long way.

"The blizzard has stopped," Luther said.

Pearl listened and smiled. "It sure has. Let me finish this here coffee and take me tonic, and we'll be off." She looked in her cup. The coffee grounds had separated. By nature a superstitious person, Pearl grabbed her plate and covered the cup. Clockwise, she swirled it three times. Tilting the cup nearer to the fire so she could read the results, Pearl waited for the grounds to settle.

The symbols started near the handle, meaning that something or someone was approaching. She continued to read around the cup. Then she saw it. A knife. Then another knife. Danger. Two knives either meant two different foes or many enemies ahead. A deep sense of foreboding filled her chest. She took one more look into the cup and saw an owl. Some hoot owl was on their trail, as well.

Pearl looked over at Luther. The poor damn fool had no idea that trouble was a-brewing, and they needed to get the hell out of that place.

"Did you hear that?" Luther asked. "I think I heard an owl."

Without a word, Pearl started packing up. She grabbed Belle's saddle and motioned for Luther to saddle his horse. Her hands were shaking. Maybe old Ida Iron Woman had had a change of heart. Blackfoot Indians were all in these parts, and Pearl figured she had overstayed her welcome. Never one to linger when she wasn't wanted, Pearl decided that she would just as soon keep her hair and not see it hanging from someone's belt.

"Pearl, what are you doing. We've just dined, and I, for one, am happy to spend the night in this nice quiet cave." He stretched and yawned. "It's out of the wind and snow." He spread his arms wide, continuing to enumerate the cavern's qualities.

"Fine by me. You stay here." Pearl cinched Belle's saddle tightly and reached for her saddlebag. "I've done seen what's in the coffee grounds, and I'm not waiting for daybreak to let it catch me."

"Coffee grounds?" He remembered her squatting by the fire with her cup. "Is that what you were doing? Reading your fortune?"

'Damn straight. I've been reading grounds, since I was a kid, and I ain't been wrong yet." She set about rolling up her bedroll. "Look, Third Luther, I'm trying to give you some good advice. Get out of here while the gettin's good."

Luther sat down on his haunches by the fire. "I think we should discuss this matter more fully. Now, Pearl, you must consider all the elements."

She slung the bedroll behind her saddle and tied it tightly. Her gaze sought out every crook and cranny of the cave, trying to see if she was leaving anything behind. She spied her bottle of Percival's Merciful Potion leaning against a rock. She reached for it and popped the cork.

"Almost forgot to take my tonic. Third Luther, we can cuss it or discuss it, but the outcome's the same. I'm getting the hell out of here."

"That tonic is nothing but alcohol. It has no medicinal value."

"Tell me about it on the trail. Move it, Luther, fore you lose your hairline."

She checked the Winchester and reloaded the Derringer. With the pistol, she pointed at Luther's holster and guns. "Them loaded?" Without waiting for an answer, she checked each gun. "You're a damn fool. These here pistols ain't even loaded. Ain't nothing going to wait for you to load." She pitched the holster to him.

He almost caught it. The guns were heavy, and the holster was filled with bullets. It dropped on the ground. Pearl shook her head like she could not believe how anyone could be so useless. Luther grabbed up the holster. Slowly, he extracted one of the revolvers and looked it over.

"You do know how to load it?"

"Yes. Yes, I do." He set the holster down. "But I don't see the need to do so at the moment."

"Well, then. I guess we're done talking, and I'm done packing."

They stood across from one another just staring at each other. So much had happened. Pearl wondered if she would ever see Luther alive again. She wanted to stay and protect him, but her instincts said the coffee grounds were right. Something wicked was out there. She could read the signs.

An owl hooted again. The sound came from the same location. Pearl knew that owls in flight called to their mates and were usually answered by the female. The Great Horned Owl usually sent out a corresponding series of hoots. This was different. The sound wasn't loud and booming; instead, it was soft almost beckoning. She swallowed hard. If she wanted to live, now was the time to high-tail it out of there.

"Luther, please get your stuff together, and let's ride."

Something in her eyes made him take a step back and reconsider. She had saved his life more than once; and if anyone had a right to his respect, it was Pearl. He nodded Without another protest, he started saddling the stallion.

Pearl picked up the holster and loaded his guns. "Put this on." She handed it to him. "You can shoot?"

"I tried them out behind the gunsmiths."

"That'll have to do." She hoped like hell he could shoot without blowing her head off. "I'll let you ride in front."

He saw her humor and laughed. "That might not be a bad idea."

Another sound echoed. This time it was the call of a wolf. Even Luther grasped that this was not a normal experience. He hurried to saddle his horse, and Pearl smothered the last dying flames of the fire, plunging the cave into darkness.

"Ready?" she asked.

"Yes."

Pearl grabbed Belle's reins and gestured for Luther to take his. Every step seemed louder. Even their breaths sounded harsh in the silence. They stepped outside the cave and stopped. Encircling the opening stood twelve Blackfoot braves.

Chapter Fourteen

Like most Blackfoot Indians, their moccasins were dyed black. Brilliant moonlight

bathed their ebony hair giving them the appearance of wearing halos. At once, Pearl recognized

the young men's resemblance to Ida Iron Woman. She realized they were Ida's sons. For a

moment, no one moved. Then, she stepped forward into the semi-circle.

"Pearl, don't!" Luther reached out and grabbed her arm, pulling her backward.

Then the fight was on. One of the younger warriors ran full force into Luther knocking

him back into the cavern. Luther pushed back, and the young warrior fell. Two of his brothers

growled low in their throats, warning Luther. But Luther was either too dumb or too afraid to

stay out of a fight. He bowed up his arms like a pugilist and started swinging.

Pearl stepped out of the way. If Third Luther wanted to get a new haircut, that was his

problem. Her? She had no beef with these men. Out of the corner of her eye, she saw Ida Iron

Woman walking out of the woods into the moonlit arena.

"*Bon jour,*" said Pearl.

"*Bon jour.*" Ida Iron Woman looked at the fight and raised an eyebrow. She looked at

Pearl, but Pearl merely shrugged.

The old woman gave a laugh and pulled a tobacco pouch from her coat. While she rolled

the smoke using a corn husk as the wrapper, Pearl retrieved her flask of whiskey from her

saddlebag. Pearl struck a hell stick against the wall of the cavern and lit the tobacco for Iron

Woman who took a deep drag and passed the cigarette to Pearl. Pearl swapped her the flask.

The cigarette tasted good, and Pearl rolled a tiny bit of tobacco around on her tongue

before spitting it out behind her. She passed the cigarette back to Ida Iron Woman and took the

flask back. Trading smokes and swigs, the two women passed an enjoyable time, watching the men punching each other. When the young'uns pushed Third Luther into the middle of the circle and started pushing him back and forth trading punches, Pearl decided that they should slow things down a bit. She looked over at Iron Woman and shook her head.

"*Arret!*" Ida Iron Woman didn't raise her voice. She didn't have to because, at once, the braves stopped fighting and moved back into formation around the cavern opening.

Luther struggled to sit up. The trampled snow had slicked over, so he fell trying to get up. He looked over at Pearl and the old Indian woman sharing their cigarette and flask. His face turned bright red, and he tried to stand up again. He flailed around but finally managed to gain an upright position, only to skate right into the group of braves. They pushed him back, and he fell flat on his rear. Everyone but Luther laughed.

Finally, one of the Blackfoot men took pity on Luther and held out his hand in support and friendship. Hoisted to his feet by the brave, Luther looked over at Pearl. She laughed and shook Ida Iron Woman's hand.

"Are you ready to go, now?" I told you we need to get out of here." Pearl mounted her horse. "I didn't expect you to play around all night."

Luther looked up at her. "You didn't mention Indians."

Pearl looked around at the warriors. They were strong able men who could have just as likely killed them as not. Without Ida Iron Woman's presence that would have been the probable outcome. She glanced over at Luther.

"I reckon I didn't. Now, if'n I was you, I'd get my rear-end up on that stallion of yours and get moving, whilst everyone is in a good mood."

As they rode forward, the braves moved aside giving them just enough room to pass through. Pearl glanced over her shoulder and saw Ida Iron Woman drinking from her silver whiskey flask. The old Indian grinned and toasted Pearl with her flask.

"Time to light a shuck out of here, Third Luther." She kicked Belle a little and set a gentle trot to the trail.

"What's the hurry? You seem to be friends with those Indians."

"Hmm. With the Blackfoot? Ida Iron Woman ain't *no* white woman's friend that I know of. She was in a good mood, and she likes her fire water. But that rock-gut whiskey ain't caught a hold of her yet, and I don't plan to be here when it does. I hear she's a mean drunk, and that flask was pretty full up. If'n she drinks all of that, she might just change her mind and decide to kill us both."

"I can't argue with that logic," Luther said.

The full moon illuminated the snow-covered landscape, turning it into a monochrome world of light and shadow. They rode through pools of brilliant light one minute and then into nooks of pitch black the next. Pearl let Belle set the pace, and they made good time as they now headed west.

Something malevolent still hovered in the air. The Blackfoot were not the danger foretold by the coffee grounds. Pearl could feel something else out there. At first, she had thought it was following them, but now she realized it was ahead. Waiting. It knew she was coming, and it didn't care. That bothered her—that someone or something disregarded her as a contender.

There were two things that Pearl wanted. She wanted her cattle, and she wanted revenge. She could not imagine Rita Lay as a true threat to her, but she couldn't totally discount the possibility. This feeling, this foreboding seemed stronger and more potent than the hate she felt for Rustlin' Rita. This felt evil.

They rode in silence. Pearl had struck a northwesterly course; and though the trail meandered a bit, it kept to the general direction. Pearl felt alive, attuned to every nuance of the landscape, every sound. The rustling of a tree limb, the call of an animal, the sound of a rock falling, churned her emotions, leaving her nerves taut and ready for action. She wasn't alone in her intuition. Belle felt it, too. The mare held herself tightly.

Luther Van Buren III was oblivious to Pearl's anxiety, and that was probably good. For Pearl did not need to shoulder his feelings. Still, it would have been nice to have someone who could share some of her worries, if only for a minute.

The trail ahead forked, and Pearl hesitated for just a moment at its head. Both paths eventually led to Brown's Hold. The wider path would take them alongside the river. The horses needed water, but the trail would leave them more exposed to anyone hiding in the cliffs above. Without moving her head, she used her peripheral vision to scan the ridges above. Nothing. Still, she felt wary. Something waited ahead. But where?

"Which way, Pearl?" Luther asked.

"Would you just hold onto your britches? I'm thinking."

"Are we lost?"

"Hell no, we ain't lost. Both roads lead to Rome, as they say. It ain't that."

She looked at him. Should she tell him that something bad waited ahead? No. He'd find out soon enough. No point in having Third Luther all jittery. Likely as not, he'd skedaddle like a jack rabbit when the shooting started.

"I'm just trying to figure out if we want to go the long way and get the horses some water or take the short road and be in Brown's Hole by the morning." She turned and looked at him. "You got any partialities here, Third Luther?"

He considered the options carefully. Even though Luther was anxious to meet his darling fiancée, he wasn't quite ready to lose Pearl's company. He didn't say this out loud, of course. For the choices Pearl had laid out had nothing to do with his feeling for Rita. They seemed to be of a more practical nature.

"I would like to make Brown's Hole in the morning, yet I fear our horses do need the water. Also, we should probably use the opportunity to clean ourselves as best as we can before we reach the settlement. Don't you think?"

"I see. You want to get all spruced up for your fiancée. Is that it?" Pearl was getting as techy as a teased snake. "Well now, you do reek like a pole-cat. That's for certain. I damn sure don't want you offending Miss Rita Odena Lay." She had another thought. "Are you implying that I stink, too?"

Luther did not say anything. He headed down the trail toward the river. Pearl followed behind, griping and cussing all the way. The trail wound through a large grove of trees and then followed the curve of the river. Bubbling and almost overflowing its banks, the river was rushing wildly along its course.

They followed its natural turns and eddies, looking for a godown in the steep bank. Pearl moved cautiously down a shallow rut in the bank. The mud was thick, but solid ground was underneath. She dismounted and motioned for Luther to bring his horse down for a drink.

Something felt wrong. Pearl looked up and down the riverbank. Trees jutted from the bank, hanging out over the water. The moon was reflected in the middle of the river like a huge spot of light on a black swirling canvas. The hairs on the back of her neck stood up. Then she heard it. A bumping sound. A scrape. She handed her reins to Luther and grabbed her Winchester.

Almost on tip-toe she eased her way down the side of the bank—clinging to roots exposed along the edge. She pushed through a tangle of overhanging vines and saw a small wooden boat caught in a knot of brush and tree roots. It kept banging and scraping against the edge of the bank. It was a rowboat carrying a dead man's body.

Chapter Fifteen

Pearl whirled and stumbled back toward Luther and the horses. Her thoughts were racing wildly, trying to figure out who the dead man was. He looked familiar, but her mind was having trouble pinning itself on any one thought. Her heart was zig-zagging around in her chest. What to tell Luther? This news would be hard to keep to herself. If she had been thinking coherently, she would have stayed and tried to get down to the boat and see if she knew the dead man. For the moment, Pearl was running scared. There was no doubt he was dead. No one alive looked that bad.

She ran alongside the riverbank looking around, behind, overhead, splashing into the water's edge. The woods felt alive with hidden dangers. Something was out there. By the time she reached Luther, she was wild-eyed and out of breath. She stood by Belle, hanging onto her neck for support. Long wheezing breaths shuddered out of her.

As soon as Pearl burst onto the godown, Luther gathered the horses' reins. For once, he didn't ask any questions. He pulled the horses back onto the trail and then went back to fetch Pearl. She hadn't moved physically, but something had shifted inside. Whatever was waiting out there for them had to be met head on. She was not some little girl playing at being a vigilante. She was a full-grown woman with a strong will and a steely determination.

Luther handed Pearl Belle's reins and waited for her to speak.

"Okay, Luther, I've got something bad I need to show you. I need you to keep your wits about you." She laughed softly. "Maybe because I am about to lose mine."

"Whatever it is, Pearl, I'm sure that it cannot be that bad."

Pearl walked a short way ahead of him on the trail, and then looked back over her shoulder at him. Her forehead was furrowed with worry.

"Oh, it's that bad alright."

After a moment, Pearl found an opening in the trees. She pulled Belle beside a juniper and tied her reins to a low-hanging branch. "You be a good girl and keep quiet."

"Third Luther, tie your horse up here by Belle. We need to get back to the water, but I don't want to leave our horses by the trail."

"Would you mind telling me what's going on?' Luther did as she asked and secured his horse alongside Belle.

As Pearl stomped back onto the trail, she said, "Trust me, Luther, this ain't easy to explain."

To Pearl, everything felt heightened. The moon shone brighter; the shadows felt darker. A sinister pall covered the night. Somewhere out there was a killer. The coffee grounds hadn't lied, and this killer had a purpose. She could feel it in her very bones. She reached behind her and grabbed Luther's hand.

Stepping carefully, they descended the muddy rut down to the river. Retracing her steps, she led him beside the river. They could hear the bumping noise growing louder. Without realizing it, Pearl gripped Luther's hand even harder. Her fingernails bit into his palm. The wind had picked up, causing the rowboat to pound into the trees mooring it to the bank. Pearl hurried.

When they rounded the corner, they could see the boat...and the dead man. His head had dropped back, and his face was ashen but bruised. He looked like he had been choked or drowned. His mouth was wide open, and his tongue hung out—mottled blue and swollen. With every beat of the boat against the shore, his body flopped back and forth. He was half-lying half-sitting in the bottom of the boat. Pearl noticed that water was starting to fill in around his legs. The boat had a leak.

"He's sinking," said Luther.

Pearl found it hard to breathe, but at that that she chuckled. "Yes, well, that ain't but half of that son of a biscuit eater's problems. Is it?"

Luther ducked around her and tried to reach the bow of the boat to haul it closer in, but the river was against him. His fingers brushed the rim but slipped off. Then the rowboat crashed into a limb, rolling closer to his hand. Just as he was about to catch it, another wave slammed into its side loosening the boat's position. It surged into the river.

"Damnation. I wanted another look at that body. It seemed his head had been crushed from the back." Luther sounded detached. Cold.

Pearl looked at him. "Yes, the butt of a rifle will do that if'n you hit someone hard enough with it."

"I wonder who that fellow was," Luther said.

The boat was high on another wave. It slammed down on the water, and the body rocked back deeper into the hull of the boat.

Pearl had finally gotten a good look at the corpse. She recognized the hombre in the rowboat. He had been a low-life scheming varmint with a soiled dove of a sister and a cattle-rustling soul. He was also as ugly as sin and a dead ringer for his two-faced thieving sibling.

"Well, Luther, I hate to be the bearer of bad tidings, but that there varmint was none other than your best man."

"What?" Luther took another look at the rowboat as it bobbed to and fro on the churning black river. Shards of moonlight ripped gashes across the surface of the water, as the dead man rode out his journey. That night the Green River was transformed, and like the River Styx, its crossing led to Hell. Luther saw something else across the river. A black shadow was moving through the trees. He stepped closer to Pearl, instinctively blocking her body from view.

Pearl leaned against a tree for support. Her arms wrapped tightly around a branch. She shuddered and laid her head on Luther's shoulder.

"That man, Luther. He was Robert Lay, your fianceé's brother. I saw him and Richard, her other brother, back in Utah just a week or so back. I heard tell that they were both headed to Brown's Hole."

Pearl did not mention that her source of information was none other than the Lay brothers themselves. At the saloon in Vernal, the pair had been slack-jawed drunk and bragging about stealing a herd of cattle. Pearl was sitting beside Ole Tickle Fingers, the piano player, so the brothers hadn't noticed her. If it had not been for Tickle Fingers, she would have jumped up and drawn down on those varmints right then and there. The old man had grabbed her arm and kept her quiet. She was grateful for that now. The saloon keeper had run those two scoundrels out of there before they could say any more, but Pearl had known that their new herd of cattle was that of her pa's.

Luther turned his head slightly. "You know Rita. Don't you?"

"We might have met." Pearl shook her head slightly. She was trying to be cagey but seeing Robert's body had unnerved her.

"You knew her brothers." He stated it as a fact.

"I told you. I saw them at the saloon in Vernal. I'm wondering where the other brother is—if'n he's still alive. They was twins and seemed to be double trouble everywhere they went."

"Why were you in a saloon?"

"Oh, Luther, I was sitting a spell. Enjoying the pi-annie."

"We need to search. Rita's other brother could be here. He could be hurt or dying."

Pearl grabbed his arm. "Luther, if'n he ain't in that boat, he's more than likely still alive. Whoever killed Robert Lay had to be after them both, or else they got in a brawl and Richard kilt him. Either way, we need to get the hell out of here."

Belle whinnied. Pear spun around—listening. "Come on, Luther. Something's spooked the horses." She tugged his arm harder now, but Luther was not moving. He was watching the shadows move across the river.

"Luther! You ain't listening to me."

But Luther was listening, and he was well aware the man across the river could hear Pearl's shrill diatribe. He pushed her behind him. With his right hand, he held her against his back. Pearl thrashed and beat against his arm. This stance put him at a direct disadvantage. He was right-handed and even though Luther was no good at shooting, he was wearing a pair of Colts. He figured he could do as well with his left hand as his right. He reached his hand as though to move an overhanging limb. When he touched the butt of his revolver, he heard the click.

The sound echoed across the river. Luther didn't stop to think. He fell to the ground, taking Pearl with him. She landed on top of him. Just as the first shot was fired, Luther rolled pinning Pearl underneath his body.

"Are you shot?" he whispered.

"Hell no, I ain't. But I'm squashed flatter than a pancake. Who the devil's shooting at us?"

"How would I know? I'm not exactly familiar with anyone except for Rita."

"Yes, and it's probably her other brother out there shooting at you, now."

"I highly doubt that, madam. My fiancée is a woman of means and mercy..."

"Your fiancée is a cattle stealing bitch, and you are as dumb as a box of rocks, if'n you think she's a high-flautin' ranch owner. On top of which you don't know nuthin' about Rita Odena Lay if you think for one second, she's the merciful kind. Why I've seen that woman slow ring a chicken's neck for the fun of hearing it squawk."

Another shot blew a limb full of juniper berries to smithereens just over Luther's head. He groaned and pushed with his legs as hard as he could. Rocks and branches scratched against them, but Luther finally scooted them behind a boulder.

"Be still, woman." He pushed Pearl out of his way and reached for his gun.

The gun was waving this way and that, and Pearl lunged for it, bringing it into her hands with one swipe. For a moment, they fought over who should use the gun. Since Luther had only fired the thing once behind the feed store, Pearl decided to take the revolver. She did not want Luther shooting holes in her while trying to defend her.

She stood and braced her body against the rock, so she could get a clean shot off. Down the sight of the Colt, she could see their attacker. Slowly, she lowered the revolver and stood still.

"What are you doing, Pearl? Shoot him."

"Hold your water. I know this man, and if'n he really wanted to kill us, we'd both be dead right now."

Luther stood up beside her.

The man across the raging waters of the river was tall and dignified. He carried himself like a gentleman, and his suit was of the finest black silk. His hat was tilted slightly giving him a devilish look. To Pearl, this man personified the devil. He was evil through and through. The man across the river was none other than Range Detective Bill Puckett. He was the meanest, most unscrupulous varmint Pearl had ever chanced to meet. Her hackles rose, and she grabbed Luther's hand to keep herself from blowing his cotton-pickin' brains out.

Bill Puckett stood another moment on the opposite side of the river. He grabbed the brim of his hat and tipped it slightly toward Pearl. Then he disappeared into the forest. Back where he came from? Or moving ahead into Pearl's future?

Chapter Sixteen

Pearl had been right about one thing. If Bill Puckett had wanted to kill them, he'd had his chance. Killing Pearl would have eliminated his competition. For Puckett was after the same prize as Pearl—Rustlin' Rita. Unbeknownst to Pearl, old man Pecker had hired Range Detective Puckett to find his cattle and to bring them back to his ranch. He had also placed a bounty on Rita's fine head and a huge reward for the return of the cattle. It was a much larger bounty than Pearl was expecting. Two hundred dollars. Dead or alive. And for the cattle? Another three hundred dollars reward.

Bill Puckett had not spared Pearl's life because he didn't cotton to killing innocent women. He had spared her because she piqued his interest. The man with Pearl was of interest to him, as well. He looked distinguished, and Puckett didn't plan to kill him, until he knew more about the fellow. But kill Luther, he would. Bill Puckett was a range detective who hired out to the highest bidder. There was no doubt in his mind that Pearl's pa would pay extra to get rid of this fancy meddler who was chasing after his daughter.

Pearl was a hindrance, but Puckett was sure that her pa wanted her kept safe. Still, he had no intention of letting a woman beat him to his bounty. Especially since that prize was the scheming, cheating Rita Odena Lay. Puckett had once been engaged to Rita when they had been nothing but kids. Kissing cousins. That damn soiled dove Rita had run off with his brother and stole his horse while she was at it. Puckett wanted to see her dead even more than Pearl did.

She had wounded his pride, but even more, she had made him a laughing-stock with his family. Well, Puckett planned to show Rita who had the last laugh. It would be him looking up her dress-tail while she danced at the end of a rope.

Bill Puckett had left Vernal a day ahead of Pearl. He had caught up with the Lay twins on their way to Brown's Hole to rejoin their sister. The two had been camped about a mile south of the territory border when Puckett had ridden past them. He had been tracking them for several days, but the blizzard had left him holed up in a make-shift lean-to for hours. Once it was over, he'd had trouble finding signs showing which way they had gone. The snow had been blowing hard enough to hide their trail. Puckett decided to ride on in the direction of Brown's Hole and catch up with them there.

Lady Luck was on Puckett's side, though, and just over a rocky hilltop, he had seen horse droppings that indicated he was probably on the right track. Around mid-afternoon, he had passed the very spot the Lay brothers had sheltered during the worst of the storm.

The twins had dug a deep pit in the snow under the boughs of a pinyon, around the trunk of the tree down to the ground. Robert had decided to pass the time smoking while they sat out the storm. Richard had just fallen asleep when Bill Puckett had smelled Robert's smoke. The pungent aroma of cheap tobacco had made him pause and scan the area more carefully.

Robert had taken a long drag of the cigarette and leaned back to look at the branches wiggling overhead. Not the sharpest rock in the box, Robert nonetheless figured out pretty quickly that the branches weren't moving on their own.

He had reached for his side arm just about the same time the branches parted, and Bill Puckett cocked his Smith and Wesson. Robert looked dead-eyed into the barrel of the pistol. It looked like a black hole leading straight to hell, and that's exactly what it was.

"I wouldn't do that if'n I was you, boy," said Bill Puckett.

"You ain't me, Pops," said Robert, but he moved his hand away from the gun.

"You aiming to get smart with me, son? Cos, if you want to go that way, I'll just blow your damn head off right here."

"No, sir." Robert had decided he might as well play along. He was at a distinct advantage.

Bill Puckett stood above him, talking as casually as if he had knelt down to tie his shoe. Robert knew better. He had heard stories about the range detective, and in all of them Puckett had come out the winner. Bill Puckett was nobody's fool. He had bushwhacked more than one outlaw.

"Wake up your brother. His snoring sounds like a hog rutting after a pig in heat." Puckett looked at the grimy pair of owl hoots. "You two smell like a herd of hogs, too. You sons of bitches ever bathe?" He wrinkled his nose in disgust.

Robert pushed and shoved on his brother's shoulders, but Richard kept on sleeping. ''Damn, boy. Wake up, brother Richard. We got trouble."

Richard turned his grubby back on his brother and farted. The putrid odor oozed and lifted. Once Bill Puckett caught a whiff of it, he stood up and walked around the top of the pit. Without a word, he moved and kicked Richard Lay straight in the forehead. Richard tumbled backward into his brother's lap. Then that varmint grabbed for his gun.

Puckett's gun was still cocked and ready. Without any ado, he blew a hole right in the center of Richard's grimy head. Robert screamed and ducked down under his brother's body. He was crying and hollering.

"Shut up, fool, fore you wake the dead—or call up a bunch of Injuns. Move that bastard out of the way and get your sorry ass up here before I decide to shoot you, too."

Bill Puckett stepped back and watched as Robert moved the bloody mess of his brother to one side. Puckett's cold dark eyes were red-rimmed, unwavering. He stroked a day's growth of beard. To all intents and purposes, he looked like a gentleman or a gambler, but Bill Puckett was a killer for hire. He hunted down the most unsavory of outlaws and either caught them or killed them. Lately, he didn't worry so much about the catching. Killing was easier and just as profitable. So, Robert Lay's future was pretty much decided. All that was left was for Puckett to determine how long Mr. Lay would stay alive.

"Throw that branch back over the hole. I'd swear your brother smells even worse dead than he did alive."

Robert scurried to obey. He spared just one last look at his twin before covering the pit they had dug just hours earlier.

"What are you planning to do with me?" Robert asked.

"Well, so, that all depends." Puckett holstered his gun, giving Robert a false sense of security. "If you tell me what I need to know, hell, I might let you go. But, if'n you want to keep silent, I'll let you join your brother there."

"What do you want to know?" Robert eased back a step or two, figuring he had a better chance at running than talking. "I might know a thing or two." He took another step back.

Bill Puckett smiled. He liked it when they ran. He enjoyed the hunt. Besides, this one would be easy. Robert Lay smelled like a dead pole cat. His scent alone would be easy to follow.

"I want to know where you have hidden my client's cattle."

Lay kept backing up. Little by little, his steps accelerated. Puckett advanced.

"Do you see any cattle around here. I ain't got nobody's cattle."

Puckett kept walking, and Lay scooted backward.

"Where's your sister? Rita." He spat out the word. "Where is Rita? I know she has the cattle. Tell me where she is."

"She might be at Brown's Hole for all I know. If'n I knew anything."

"Brown's Hole is a mighty big place," said Puckett. "I want to know exactly where she is."

"I'll bet you do," yelped Robert. He took off running and slipping through the trees, moving toward the river. Once he reached the river, he could get away. He and Richard had a rowboat tied to some roots just past the godown. They used the rowboat to haul feed and supplies up the river to their camp at Brown's Hole. He planned to jump in that boat and let the current take him the hell away from the range detective.

Bill Puckett wasted little time in his pursuit. His movements were like those of the most dangerous predator—swift and silent. He pursued his quarry relentlessly. As Robert floundered in the drifts of snow, Puckett waded through and still came after him. His steps were long and certain.

Robert reached the trace that led down to the water and the rowboat. It was steep and covered with ice. When his foot hit the first slick spot, he fell on his rear and slid the rest of the way down to the river.

Puckett was right behind him. Moving faster now. Holding to limbs and branches for support, but still moving steadily along. He didn't make a sound, but Robert could feel him gaining.

Robert reached the rowboat and hurried to untie it from its moorings. His fingers were swollen with cold and clumsy with fear. He could sense his attacker right behind him. He fumbled once more, trying desperately to loosen the knot. A hand touched his shoulder. Robert cried out and spun around, trying to hit Puckett in the face.

Puckett dodged the hit and laughed. The sound stabbed Robert in the heart. Puckett's hands reached around Robert's throat and started choking him. He pushed his thumbs across Robert's larynx, crushing it. Robert heard the crackle and tried to cry out. Nothing.

Puckett was smiling. Robert realized that he didn't care if he talked or not. Nothing would save him now. Puckett would kill him. When he found Rita, he would kill her, too. With one last effort, Robert pulled his gun. The shot went wild. He missed.

Fury exploded in Bill Puckett's eyes. He grabbed Robert's pistol and then threw him facedown into the hull of the boat. As Robert struggled to get up, Puckett raised the barrel of the pistol high above Robert's head. With an oath, he brought it down, crushing Robert's skull.

Dispassionately, Bill Puckett shoved Robert's legs into the boat. He righted the body as though it was going for a ride. Then he untied the rope and kicked the boat into the water. He tipped his hat, turned on his heel and left.

Robert Lay's rowboat floated about a foot away from the bank. Then the river grabbed it and slammed it back against the bank. It wedged into some tree roots growing out of the bank where it scraped and bumped, until Pearl found it.

Chapter Seventeen

"Why didn't you shoot him while you had the chance? I don't understand you at all, Pearl. You had him in your sights, and you let him walk away. What if he's behind us right now? Waiting for the opportunity to kill us like he did poor Rita's brother."

Pearl was not listening to Luther. She was hell bent on getting back to Belle. She figured that since Bill Puckett was on the other side of the river, he had about an hour's head start on them. Fording the river when it was so swollen wasn't possible, so she knew he had ridden up to the only place possible to cross over—Jensen's Bridge. Jensen's Bridge wasn't a man-made bridge. It was a natural arch of rock about four feet wide that spanned the river at one of its most narrow points.

The only problem with using the bridge was trying to get the horses to climb up onto it. The way up was at least twenty feet from the ground, and it was a curving nightmare of a trail when it was dry. Covered with snow, the path would be harrowing. Still, it was the quickest way to catch up with Puckett.

They could easily backtrack a mile and go back to the deer trail and then go through the canyon but doing so would give Bill Puckett a day's head start on them. Pearl had figured out who Puckett was really after. He was after Rustlin' Rita. She would die before that skunk bait got his hands on Rita and her pa's cattle. That bounty was hers, and no black-hearted son of a biscuit eater was going to take it from her.

"Come on, Third Luther. There's only one thing for it, and we've got to move these critters up onto that bridge yonder and back down again. We may be riding into Bill Puckett's dust, and we'll be close enough behind him to choke on it."

"Who is this Bill Puckett person? And why didn't you shoot him? You haven't answered my question."

"I haven't answered your questions, because you're asking too damn many of them. Bill Puckett is the lowest, meanest belly-crawler in the West. He's also one of the fastest gunslingers I've ever seen. Once he got of prison down in Yuma, he declared himself reformed and became a range detective. Said it took a thief to catch a thief, and he ain't been wrong about that."

Pearl dismounted and marched toward Jensen's Bridge. Luther followed her, and still he kept asking questions. "What does this have to do with us? Are we following him?"

Pearl walked on. "It don't have nothing to do with *us*, but it's got everything to do with me. I'm on the trail of a thieving cattle rustler who took off with my pa's herd, and now it seems that Bill Puckett is after the same varmint. I'm a sworn-in vigilante, and I ain't about to let someone else get the money and the glory for catching that crook."

They were almost to the bridge. In the moonlight, Pearl could see Puckett's tracks. She could make out where his horse had almost slid off the edge of the ascent. She tightened her lips and concentrated on finding the safest way up to the ledge.

Then Pearl noticed more tracks. Puckett had two other horses with him, but these tracks were lighter than his. He was leading these horses. No riders. For Pearl the question of whether or not Bill Puckett had killed both Lay brothers was answered. Briefly, she wondered where the other body was. Puckett did not need it to collect the bounty, though. The reward was for Rustlin' Rita alone.

"Pearl, who do you think stole your father's cattle? You truly don't think Rita's brothers had anything to do with that crime. Do you?"

"Shut up, Third Luther. I sure as hell don't want to discuss this right now."

Pearl walked about a third of the way up the path to the top, stomping down loose snow and cutting ruts in the ice with her heel. She tried to make the way up less slippery.

"Pearl, you know as well as I do that Rita's brothers would have no need to be involved in such a scandal. My word, their sister is one of the largest lady cattle ranchers in the West."

"She's large, all right." Pearl guffawed. "Watch how you step, Luther, and pay attention. We got all day tomorrow to talk, but I hope you won't. First things first. Let's get these horses over this bridge and get our tails on the road to Brown's Hole."

Every step up the slippery precipice was nerve-wracking. Slowly, patiently, Pearl coaxed Belle up to the top of Jensen's Bridge. She worried about the surface of the bridge. If the rock was covered with ice, they could easily plunge to their death in the river below. Still, she knew that Bill Puckett and his horses had crossed over. She had seen him on the other side. So, she kept going.

Once at the top, Pearl was happy to see the way was clear. The wind had swept the rock bridge clear of snow, and though it was cold, it was safe enough to cross. At the summit, Pearl stopped and looked out over the river. The full moon gleamed brightly, lighting up the night. Below them, the river was a glistening black snake surrounded by brilliant jewels. Pearl could see for miles, but what she didn't see worried her the most. She did not see hide nor hair of Bill Puckett.

Luther and the stallion followed Belle across the bridge. Even though the surface of the bridge had been dry, the way down was slick as glass. Just before Pearl and the mare made it to the bottom, Luther's horse started to slip.

"Whoa, whoa, watch out!" Luther yelled.

It was too late. Luther and the stallion careened down the slope right into Pearl and Belle. Luther's stallion knocked Belle flat. Pearl went head over heels, tumbling toward the river.

Swollen watery jaws clamped around her legs, and Pearl was almost dragged into the raging current. The water was so cold. At first, it took Pearl's breath away. She struggled against the weight of her skirt. It was pulling her down. Pearl never let anything take the advantage over her. Not a man. Not even the river. She turned onto her belly and clawed her way back onto the bank. She was madder than a nest full of hornets and wet from the waist down.

Luther ran to help her, but she slapped his hand away. Her mouth was drawn up tight to keep her teeth from chattering. The sodden swag of her skirt slapped against her legs as she fought to stand upright.

"Luther Van Buren III, keep away from me. You and your jackass of a horse have got to be the dumbest, clumsiest creatures in all of nature. If'n you don't burn us down, get us scalped, or starve us to death, you'll just shove me in the river. I don't believe it."

Luther didn't say a word. He looked at Pearl. Her hair was flying wild around her face like a witch's halo. She was beautiful but furious, and her eyes held nothing for him but disdain. He scratched the back of his neck, and then he got on his horse and rode away.

"Fine, you pole cat. Ride off." Pearl yanked at the tie on her skirt, until it came loose. As she slithered and shook out of her soaking wet long skirt, she yelled after him. "Get on with you, then. Shoo. Shoo." She wrung out the skirt and stomped to Belle's side and hung onto the stirrup, while she dragged her trousers down around her ankles. Still yelling, she kicked at first one and then the other, trying to get them off. Her feet were frozen and had started to go numb.

Luther urged the stallion into a trot. He was headed for the river bend. Soon he would be out of sight.

"Lily-livered son of a biscuit eater. Leaving a poor defenseless woman to take care of herself," she hollered. She got her foot free of the boot, but the other was stuck tight. Madder than she had ever been in her life, Pearl grabbed her Winchester from the saddle and fired a shot at Luther.

The bullet nipped the very top of his hat, blowing it high into the air above Luther's head. He stopped. Slowly, deliberately, he turned the horse around. Then he kicked the horse into a full gallop. Snow and stones flew behind the stallion's hooves. He barreled down on Pearl, barely stopping at her side.

She stood there. Bare-legged and shivering. Feeling triumphant and afraid all at the same time. Luther jumped down from the horse and grabbed her up.

"Luther! Luther. Put me down."

He held her tightly against him, while he pulled her bedroll from her horse. Without saying a word, he threw Pearl over his shoulder and carried her to a clearing away from the froth of the river. He tossed the bedroll onto the ground and then dumped Pearl on top of it.

"Luther! You low-life..."

"Pearl. Be quiet and dry yourself off. Then cover up with that blanket before you catch your death of cold."

Pearl sputtered, but one look from Luther shut her up. For once, she decided she had better hold her tongue. Even though she was madder than a wet setting hen, Pearl figured that Luther was right about one thing at least. She was cold as ice and feeling weaker by the minute. She needed to warm up and regain her fortitude. There was no telling what kind of trouble they would land in if Third Luther was in charge.

Chapter Eighteen

Morning was still hours away, and Pearl was feeling as worn out as a rag doll in a house full of children. Trying to stand and cover her quaking legs was almost more than she could manage. Luther watched her efforts for a few minutes and then came over to help. He shook out the bedroll and blanket and wound Pearl up in them like she was no more than a papoose. Then, gently, he scooped her up in his arms and carried her to rest under the shelter of an overhanging rock.

Great chills racked her body. Without realizing what she was doing, Pearl clung to Luther. Her arms were wrapped tightly around his neck. She was cold to the bone, and it felt like she would never be warm again.

"We need to keep going, Luther," she whispered. "Puckett will get there before us and take Pa's cattle."

"Shhh. We can't go anywhere at the moment. You must warm up, and then we can be on our way. We will just rest here until morning."

"Morning? But that's hours away."

"No, it will be here soon." He patted her hair as though she was a little child. "Sleep now. Shhh. Just close your eyes."

Finally, Pearl fell asleep. Even asleep she was still shivering, so Luther laid her back against the soft sand and massaged her legs and feet through the blanket. Eventually, her body regained its heat and became still. Luther pulled Pearl close, curled up beside her, and went to sleep.

Pearl awoke to a beautiful sunrise and the smell of burning coffee. Third Luther was cooking again. Tarnation. She figured that Luther could burn water instead of boiling it, if he wasn't careful. She smiled and stretched with the joy of being young and alive. And warm. Pearl realized that she was not longer bone-chilling cold. Her blankets felt solid and safe. For a moment, she allowed herself the luxury of wallowing in their warmth.

All good things must come to an end, though, and finally Pearl had to emerge from her cotton cocoon and get dressed. When the cold morning air hit her legs, Pearl wanted nothing more than to scamper back under those covers and spend the day, but there was a devil man out there...and a soiled dove named Rustlin' Rita. Laying up on her fanny all day wasn't going to get her cattle back.

"Luther," Pearl called.

Luther was gone. The coffee was bubbling on a low fire, but Luther was nowhere to be seen. Pearl jumped up from the bedroll and looked around for her trousers. They were just above her, stretched alongside her skirt on a flat rock to dry. She put on the cold, stiff pants and hobbled over river rocks to the fire to rescue the coffee and take the chill off her bones.

Pearl poured a cup of the muddy black stew and blew on the coffee to cool it. Still, she didn't see Luther. His horse was tethered beside Belle, so he couldn't have gone far. Her heart skipped a beat. What if Bill Puckett had come back while they were asleep? Pearl decided that it would be just like that varmint to kill off Luther and narrow the competition.

Without thinking, she yanked on her skirt and boots and saddled up the horses. Visions of Luther lying wounded or dead in the new fallen snow blinded Pearl to her own mortality. She never stopped to think that if Bill Puckett would have wanted to kill off his competitors, he could have started with her.

"Luther?" she yelled just once more. She almost fainted when his voice boomed behind her.

"What are you caterwauling about, madam? Your voice is echoing throughout this canyon."

She whirled around. "Luther, I couldn't find you." She looked him up and down. "Someone did the spit and polish. I guess you decided to get gussied up before we reach Brown's Hole."

Luther had washed up and shaved. Compared to Pearl's dishevelment, he looked every inch the English gentleman. With her tangled hair and wrinkled clothes, Pearl looked more like an urchin child than a grown woman. Beside Luther, she felt increasingly shabby.

"I am expecting to meet my fiancée today." He coughed, suddenly feeling uncomfortable. "I've always found it expedient to make a good first impression."

Pearl snorted. "Yeah, I'll never forget my first impression of you. Face down in the snow coughing and gagging." She yanked the brush from his hand and marched away down the bank.

"I'll just have some coffee, while you make your repairs," he said.

"You do that," she muttered.

During the night, the weather had changed. Warmer and brighter, this new day promised clear skies and a bright sun. The water twinkled, reflecting the trees overhead. Flashes of color swirled and glowed with the ever-running river. Huge clay boulders rimmed the bank. Pearl hopped from rock to rock, until she came to one that jutted out over the river and afforded her access to the water. She lay belly-down on the rock and scooped handfuls of cold, clear water to wash her face and neck.

A slight breeze stung her cold wet cheeks, drying them and leaving her face clean and pink. She sat up and loosened her hair. The wind lifted her curls and swirled them every which way. Pearl fought to tame them with the brush. Strand by strand, she untangled her locks and smoothed them into a bun at the base of her neck. Finally, she stood and brushed down her clothes and stomped the mud off her boots.

She walked back to the campfire and handed Luther the brush. "That'll just have to do," she said. "You can't make a silk purse from a sow's ear."

Luther smiled. "I say you look quite nice this morning. Bright-eyed and ready to go."

Pearl nodded, thinking that Third Luther was a few bricks short of a load. Out of her innate politeness, she decided to hold her tongue.

"I, for one, am very excited today. I will finally get to meet my intended. I have traveled far and waited for this moment with great anticipation."

Pearl's hackles rose, but then she thought of Luther's reaction when he would finally meet his "intended." She almost felt sorry for him.

"Yeah, that's going to be some meeting."

Pearl thought of the last time she had seen Rustlin' Rita dressed up. She had gone into town to pick up some supplies, and Rita and some cowpoke had staggered out of the Vernal saloon. Rita had looked a sight—stuffed into a shiny blue dress three sizes too small for her. Pearl recalled that Rita had drawn a red rouge circle on each cheek, giving her the appearance of a fancy doll. Pearl was fairly certain that Luther Van Buren III was not ready to meet his fiancée. Unless she was mistaken, Luther had no idea who he was about to meet.

Chapter Nineteen

The beauty of the morning invited nature to fully awaken and stretch her wings. After the bitterness of the blizzard, creatures great and small decided to take a break from their winter naps and enjoy the sun. The trees were alive with birds. As Pearl and Luther rode alongside the river toward the gates of Lodore, they saw yellow warblers and bright orange orioles with their black and white-tipped wings. One industrious fellow had found something to eat. He was swinging it back and forth in his beak. Pearl could not tell what he was eating, but the notion of an early morning breakfast soon had her searching the riverbank for animal tracks. Her stomach felt like a tight knot, and Luther's coffee had not helped her hunger at all.

"We're almost to the canyon, Luther. Once we leave the river, the traveling will be pretty much uphill for a while. When we top the largest crest, we will go through the gates. The river cuts right through the mountains."

"What is the river?" Luther asked. He had never seen a river so broad and wild.

"Damn, Luther. You don't even know where you are? This here's the *Seeds-ke-dee-Agie*, at least that's what the Blackfoot call it."

"The what?"

"*Seeds-ke-dee-Agie.* That means prairie hen in proper English. Some folks call it the Green River."

Pearl spotted a pinyon with a few nuts left on it. With a whoop and a holler, she rode for it. The nuts were old, and their shells had not fully opened, but she was too hungry to care. She grabbed a handful, shucked them and stuffed one in her mouth. Then she shoved a couple at Luther.

"Here. Eat these, whilst I scout around for some game. We've got to have something to eat. We're about to pass through the reddest mountains you've ever seen. I, for one, don't intend to do it on an empty stomach."

Pearl rode on ahead, while Luther brushed the powdery snow from the tree and picked every pinyon nut he could find. The underside of the small tree yielded more of the savory nuts, and he filled his pockets. About ten yards from the stand of trees, Pearl spotted the makings of a campfire and the remains of an antelope carcass. Even though she was ravenously hungry and the meat was still edible, she was furious. Only a wastrel would abandon such a feast.

"Luther, over here."

She set about stoking up the fire. With her knife, she began to strip off the animal's hide and expose the flesh beneath.

"What in God's name?" Luther was clearly repulsed by the sight. "Are these some animal's leavings? I'm not sure that I can eat them. You've no idea how long that meat has been exposed."

"You're right." Pearl took a hind quarter and sniffed it. "Smells good to me." She gestured to her saddlebag. "Get my pan, Third Luther, and start some coffee brewing, while I get us some meat cooking. And don't burn the coffee this time. Hellfire just boil the water, and I'll do the rest. If'n you don't want to partake, that's fine by me, but I ain't got a store of vitals in that saddlebag yonder." Pearl's meaning was clear—eat or starve.

Her knife was sharp and soon long strips of meat slid from the bone and were sizzling over the fire. Luther did as he was told and started some coffee. As much as he wanted to protest, the smell of the meat cooking had his stomach singing for joy.

"Are the leftovers from an Indian's meal? Should we be on the lookout for savages?" Luther asked.

"No Indian I ever met would've left this antelope for the critters or to ruin. In these parts, the Utes and the Blackfoot use every bit of an animal. Nothing is left to waste. I'd wager it was Puckett what left this, and that tells me more about that varmint that I don't like."

Luther looked again at the simmering meat. "Are you sure the meat is fine? What kind of animal is this?"

"Hells bells, Third Luther, you cain't even recognize an antelope?" She looked at the small pile of leftover skin and bones. "Any fool can tell what that is. And, yes, the meat should be fine. It's colder than blue blazes out here. It's a wonder it ain't frozen solid."

The implications of what she had just said hit Pearl like a flash. This could be a trap. She grabbed her Winchester and circled the campsite looking for traces of Puckett. The fire ring was exposed and built on a rock. There were no tracks, no footprints around it. Foot by foot, she widened the perimeter of her search. The rock face showed scuffs and scratches but effectively hid any footprints. Finally, when she was about ten feet out toward the canyon gates, she spied an area that had clearly been stomped down by horses. Crouching down, she examined the spot and then followed its trail into the mouth of the canyon. Sure enough, three horses had been tethered to a nearby tree.

"That polecat has definitely been this way." She turned and looked at Luther. "He must have rested here a bit, though. Them tracks are fresh, and the extra horses sure as hell won't slow him down. He'll be in Brown's Hole in no time. He can switch out and have a fresh horse every few hours."

"Coffee's ready," Luther said. "I'm starving, and this meat looks delicious."

Pearl's stomach rumbled in agreement. "You're right. Let's eat and then we can be after Puckett. A full belly is what we need right now to keep going. That's for sure and certain."

"Once we arrive at my darling Rita's ranch, we can surely have any matter of beef. She wrote in her letters that she has at least a hundred cattle.

Red flashed through Pearl's eyes, but Luther was too bent on eating the antelope to notice. Rustlin' Rita had better forget about cooking a barbeque once Pearl got to Brown's Hole. The very idea of Rita butchering one of the Pecker herd made Pearl so mad she wanted to blast Rita into oblivion. She could have stomped a mudhole in Rita right then and there. Pearl vowed that if there was any roasting to be done, it would be her roasting Rita's fat ass over a flaming campfire. Mentally, she pictured Rita all gussied up and hanging from a spit. Yep, that Rita was dead meat and that was for damn sure.

To Luther she said, "That Rita's a braggart, ain't she?" Always a goin' on about what she's got and how."

"Now see here, Pearl. Rita was merely sharing her good fortune with me. Once we're married, what is mine will be hers and what's hers will be mine."

Pearl's lips drew tightly together. And what's mine, I'll be taking back, and then what's hers is going to be mighty scarce, she thought. Aloud, she said, "I hear you, Third Luther." She narrowed her eyes. What if Luther was behind Rita's rustling scheme?

Sidling up next to him, she cocked her head and looked at him from under her lashes. "Where do you think your fiancée got all them cattle from, Third Luther? Did a rich relative keel over and will them to her and them rascal brothers of hern?"

Luther looked puzzled. "I've never thought to ask. Pearl, it is considered rude to question how someone procures their wealth. However, I am sure a woman like my dear Rita Lay was either bequeathed her herd or perhaps she earned them."

Pearl snorted. "In these parts, a woman gets a herd of cattle like that in two ways. She either steals them, or she beds with someone who did."

"That's enough. You don't know my fiancée like I do, and I'm certain that she's a woman of fine moral character. I will not have you besmirch her name." Luther started wiping out the frying pan and putting out the fire.

As Pearl wrapped the remainder of the meat in a cloth, she studied Luther's face. One glance told her he was furious, and for a moment she wondered what it would feel like to have someone so indignant on her behalf. Then she shook the notion away. Third Luther was in for a shock. She almost felt sorry for him. Almost.

"You're right as rain, Mr. Van Buren. I owe you an apology. A woman oughtin' to show disrespect for another's intended." She mocked a curtsey. "My excuses."

Luther studied Pearl's face. It was smooth and guile free. She did not look terribly sorry. On the other hand, she did look wistful. Maybe that was enough.

Chapter Twenty

The Gates of Lodore Canyon opened to a stunning view of the Green River and the towering Uinta Mountain Group rock formation. Capped with snow, the red quartzite walls of the mountain offered a dramatic backdrop to the canyon. The trail ahead of them had obviously been recently traveled. Puckett's tracks were evident along the way. Once the wind picked up though, the snow blew this way and that obscuring most of his traces.

Pearl was not too worried about ricing up on Puckett. Instead, she fretted that he would get to Brown's Hole before her and take her pa's cattle before she had her chance to get them back. Taking a herd of cattle from Rita was one thing, getting them from Puckett would be another. Rita was a female polecat and mean as a she-grizzly, but Bill Puckett was known to be one of the most ruthless men in the West.

Slapping leather against Puckett had meant death for more than one hombre. While Pearl had no soft feelings against shooting Puckett, she had no illusions, either. In a shootout with him, Pearl didn't stand a chance. She needed to beat him to Rustlin' Rita, and she needed help to do it. She wanted to rescue those cattle and be long gone before Puckett got wind of it.

Luther led his stallion to the edge of the river to drink. Pearl followed close behind. The horses needed their fill of water, and so did she and Luther. Rocks covered with sludge and spray made a naturally slippery dock. Pearl dismounted and carefully led Belle close to the water.

"Luther, this here river was run years back by a trapper name of General William Ashley. He must have been some kind of cuss to ride the rapids through these mountains. This ain't no easy water. There's bound to be ten or twelve patches that'd stand a girl's hair up for years to come.

Luther looked at the wide twisting river in front of them. Water hit huge rocks and spewed high into the air. "A man would have to be either courageous or crazy to try this river."

Pearl laughed and nodded in agreement. "I'll wager that General fellow was a bit of both. You reckon?"

Luther reckoned.

Pearl swung up into her saddle and angled away from the raging waters. Once Belle's hooves hit the trail, they eased into a trot and headed for the bluffs ahead. There had to be a shortcut through the mountains. If Pearl was going to move ahead of Puckett, this was the place to do it.

The only shortcut she knew of was just north of where the rock began to change from quartzite to sandstone and limestone layers. The mountains there contained all sorts of trails and outlaw hideouts. Once such trail had often been used by Butch Cassidy and his gang.

"Luther, I'd feel better if'n we didn't run into that Puckett fellow again," Pearl said.

"So would I. But if we're headed to the same place as he is, we are sure to come upon him—unless he reaches Brown's Hole before we do."

"Too true, Third Luther." Pearl had decided the best way to keep Luther on her side against Bill Puckett was to play up Puckett's dangerous character. "I'm just thinking that if that varmint killed Rita's brother, he most likely will be after her next."

It was clear that Luther had not thought of that possibility. He sat up straighter on his horse, learning forward and looking over the landscape.

"I'm thinking we are going to have to ride the high lines and beat that rascal to Brown's Hole," said Pearl.

"What are the High Lines? Where are they?" Luther looked up at the bluffs on either side.

Pearl pointed ahead to a small trail winding through the sandstone mountains ahead. It rose steeply, hugging the edge of the mountain. "I know you're thinking that trail would make a mountain goat nervous, and you would be right. But we ain't got no other choice. If'n we are going to save your darlin', we need to make time and make it fast."

As they approached the winding trail, they could see how small and rock-strewn it really was. As Pearl forged ahead, Luther reined in and studied the face of the bluff.

"This look as though we'll have to travel awfully slow to get across it. Are you sure this won't take more time than sticking to the trail here?"

"You do what you want. We're wasting time jawin' over this." Pearl slapped her hand against Belle's shoulder and up she went. The trail was bumpy and hard to follow in most places, but Pearl knew that once they made it to the other side, the going was bound to get much easier.

Reluctantly, Luther followed. He brought up the rear slowly and carefully. His horse was not as sure-footed as Pearl's mare. It was skittish, and the going didn't get easier. In fact, it got harder with every turn. Luther was about to give up, but there was nowhere to turn. The narrow trail stretched out high ahead of them, and they had no way of knowing what waited over the next ridge.

When Pearl capped the crest, the wind just about blew her back over to the other side. Great gusts of wind slapped against the sandstone, dislodging rocks and snow that pelted down on rider and horse. Pearl pulled up Belle's head turning it to one side to avoid the stones. The result was that Belle stumbled to the other side thinking that Pearl wanted her to turn.

The pair wobbled close to the rim of the trail. Falling would plunge them hundreds of feet to their deaths. Pearl pulled back harder on the reins and leaned her body back counter to the movement of the horse. Belle shied back, and with that one movement brought them to flatter ground. The struggle had cost Pearl time and energy. She moved carefully around the next bend.

Even though Pearl was a superb horsewoman, nothing had prepared her for what was ahead. Chet Miller, an hombre so dastardly that he had killed his own mother and stolen her horse, was lying in wait. He was on the run from Brown's Hole, where even other outlaws found him a vermin-soaked varmint that needed a noose for a necktie. Chet had seen Pearl and Luther, before they had approached the trail. He had backtracked and laid his trap. Tying a piece of rope from one side of the trail to the other, he had formed a trap. As Belle picked carefully down the path, she caught her hoof on the rope and stumbled forward. She pitched Pearl headfirst over the edge of the bluff.

Pearl screamed. The shrill cry rent the otherwise tranquil morning. The wind caught her cry and echoed it through the mountains. One the trail below, Luther urged his horse to move faster.

Chet Miller grinned down at Pearl, as she clung to a scrap of brush protruding from the side of the mountain. His yellow teeth were crusted over, and Pearl was at least grateful she didn't have to smell his breath. Her foot found a hold, and she flattened her belly against the rock face.

Chet knelt and glared at her from the periphery of the trail. "Do I know you? You look familiar. Ain't you a Pecker?"

Pearl's shoulders felt like they were about to pop out of their sockets. Just what she needed an examination about her family. "My pa's a Pecker." She shifted, and her foot slipped. She clung even tighter to the tenacious little scrub bush.

"Help me up. What are you after me for?" She pulled with all her might, trying to ease up the rock.

"Maybe I want your horse. She's a pretty filly." He looked back at Pearl. "Horse like her fetches a good price. Might get some double eagles for her, or I might just keep her and sell the stallion, once I kill that fellow with you."

They could both hear Luther coaxing the stallion forward.

"I'll kill you first."

Chet laughed and spit over the side of trail.

"Luther, go back!" Pearl screamed. "Go back. It's a trap!"

Chet drew his pistol and headed down the trail on foot. Pearl's voice echoed through the mountains. Only the surging river kept Bill Puckett, only minutes below, from hearing her call.

Down the trail, Luther stopped his horse and eased down to the ground. His guns seemed wedged into their holsters. He could see Chet easing around slabs of limestone. The brim of his hat jutted out just below an outcropping. Finally, Luther yanked one pistol free, accidentally firing it overhead. The bullet hit hard into the cluster of rock. Chet was close to the rock wall. Rocks exploded into the air, raining down on Chet's head just as he was about to shoot. One large rock rolled down the face of the bluff and struck Chet on the shoulder. He went down.

In the meantime, Pearl pulled herself up the cliff. Each protrusion of rock provided a grip or a toe hold. Inch by inch, she climbed up the side until she reached the summit. Her arms ached, but still she pulled. Belle was waiting at the top. She fastened her huge teeth onto Pearl's jacket and tugged with all her might, pulling Pearl onto the trail. Sighing, Pearl fell onto her back. Belle nudged her stomach with her nose, and then gave Pearl's face a lick.

Pearl wrapped her arms around the mare's head and allowed the mare to pull her to her feet. The Winchester was still in its hold on the saddle, but Pearl had no intention of causing an avalanche. She grabbed her knife, testing the solidness of its weight.

She staggered from fatigue. Pumping her shoulders back and forth and then up and down, trying to get the feeling and strength back into them, Pearl made her way around the curve of the rock. That's when she saw Chet Miller rising to his feet. Ahead of him, Luther struggled to free his other gun.

Pearl sighed. Luther was more likely to blow his own foot off than to shoot the outlaw— if he managed to free the Colt at all. Chet went to draw down on his prey. With a battle holler that would make a Blackfoot proud, Pearl launched her body into the air straight at Chet's back.

Too late, the desperado whirled around. Pearl brought her knife down on him, cutting into his side. He hit at her with his pistol. She pulled the knife back and stabbed him again. This time the blade plunged into his chest.

Chet fell away from her. He grabbed the handle of the knife, trying to yank it out. He was too late. Frothy, red bubbles foamed from his mouth. He wheezed like a squeeze box running out of air. His eyes rolled back into their sockets. Chet fell back. Dead.

Chapter Twenty-One

Chet Miller's body twitched just once, before it went still. His eyes stared blindly at nothing. This man had killed his own kin and had tried to kill Pearl and Luther. Pearl could not dredge up so much as a tear. She placed her fingers on his eyelids, shutting them forever.

"What are we going to do?" Luther asked as Pearl as Pearl stood and headed back to Chet's horse. "We can't just leave him here."

"No, we cawn't," Pearl mocked Luther's accent. She grabbed the horse's reins and led him back to the body. Chet's horse, the one he had stolen from his mother, was a fine buckskin. Pearl had no intention of leaving it or Chet's body behind. If she was right, there was a bounty on Mr. Chet Miller, and she figured she might as well collect it.

"Get his guns and check his pockets for anything that might fall out on the trail, cos this polecat ain't going to be sitting astride. There's no point in leaving a path of his belongings."

Chet's body was still warm, and Luther forced himself to touch it. Gingerly, he lifted the dead man's coat. His fingers moved around the knife still protruding from Chet's chest to rifle through his shirt pocket.

"He ain't going to bite you, Third Luther," said Pearl. "Hey, grab my knife while you're at it." She had pulled one of Chet's saddlebags open. It was filled with hard tack and venison jerky. Pearl smelled the jerky. It wasn't rank. She moved it to her own saddlebag.

Blood covered the handle of Pearl's knife, and Luther didn't want to pull it out. With the tip of his index finger, he jiggled the handle. It was stuck fast.

"For God's sake," said Pearl. She reached across the body and jerked on the knife handle. It barely moved. "Now ain't that something. I must've hit something solid. I know damn well it weren't his heart." She stood and put her foot on his chest. "Cos this owl hoot didn't have one."

Using both hands, she snatched the knife free. Pearl gathered up her skirt-tail and wiped the blade clean. The blood on her hands was sticky. She had to pour water from Chet's canteen to clean it off.

"Now, Pearl, you don't know that..."

"To hell I don't. That son of a biscuit eater told me outta his own measly mouth that he killed his mother. If that bastard had a heart, it had shriveled up like a peach pit."

Together, they hoisted the body over the back of his horse and tied him on. Pearl did not want him sliding off. Taking care of this business was taking up way too much time.

The sun was high overhead when they resumed their trek. Pearl kept the outlaw's horse between Belle and Luther's stallion. Luckily, the buckskin was a good horse. He didn't seem to mind that his cargo was riding face-down instead of right-side up.

Once they came down from the steep side of the bluff, the trail broadened and flattened out. Pearl let Belle have her head, and they moved into an easy gallop that erased the time lost dealing with Chet. It wasn't long before the trio made it to the steep canyon that led into Brown's Hole. The Hole was an isolated, grassy valley circled by mountains.

Traversing the canyon was uneventful. Pearl, for one, was grateful. The trip to Brown's Hole had been treacherous enough, and she used the time it took to get through the canyon to marshal her strength and to make a plan. Bill Puckett was somewhere in Lodore Canyon behind her. Rustlin' Rita was ahead. Pearl was going to have to act smart and work fast. Somehow, she didn't think that Third Luther was going to be much help with either adversary. Luther might be the handsomest man she had ever laid eyes on, but he was damn useless when it came to almost anything else.

Once they cleared the canyon, they came upon Lockjaw Lemmings' Trading Post. It was a sorry looking enough building built of clay and wood. The roof timbers sagged in the middle, and the porch was crusted over with mud and sludge.

"Lordy mercy, that place looks sadder than a mule pulling an ugly old maid's wagon. Neither she nor it stands a chance of a happy ending," said Pearl.

Pearl and Luther reined in and tied their horses at the rough-hewn hitching rail in front of the trading post. It was afternoon, and nary a soul was stirring. Something felt off. Pearl looked both ways before she set foot on the porch. Next to the swinging door of the trading post was a wanted poster featuring none other than Mr. Chet Miller. Pearl laughed, and neither Luther nor Chet appreciated her humor. Dead or alive. She thanked goodness for that.

"Luther," she looked back at him as she pulled her Winchester from her saddle, "draw that gun of yours, and at least look like you could shoot something."

She pointed at the wanted poster and walked over to rip it from the wall. "Some hardcase might try to relieve us of our passenger, so I need you to guard the body, until I get his bounty."

Luther slid beside the corpse of Chet Millerand stood with his gun drawn and the brim of his hat pulled low. "I'll do it, but please hurry up. I have come a long way. First a stage to Denver and then the ride out West. Finally, I met you. Since then, I've thought of nothing save my beautiful love. I can't wait to surprise her."

Pearl stopped and whirled around. "She's not expecting you?" She couldn't keep the exhilaration out of her voice.

"Oh, she's expecting me. In fact, I was supposed to arrive three days ago. Then I met you, and the blizzard changed everything. So, I'm sure she'll be surprised."

"What's that?" Luther asked.

Pearl ignored him and went inside the trading post to claim her money. The interior of the store was dark and smelled dank. A tall greasy-looking fellow was behind the counter. Pearl was instantly on her guard. Still, she marched up to the counter and laid the poster on it.

"You the man to talk to about collecting my money?"

The fellow behind the wood-slab countertop laughed and spit a stream of tobacco juice into a spittoon on the floor beside him. "I might be. Don't tell me that you've got Chet Miller out there."

"I sure do. You did say dead or alive?"

"Why? That polecat dead?"

Pearl turned and walked to the door. Outside, Luther was surrounded by a group of hardcases. Some of the bunch happened to be Chet's cousins. They had never much liked Chet, but he was family. If anybody was going to collect on Chet's dead body, they figured it might as well be them.

"Chet's blood has all run to his head," said the tallest of the owl hoots, who also happened to be Chet's third cousin Chick.

"Yep, but it don't look that bad. Hell, Chet's so ugly. He don't look no worse," said Chick's younger brother. "In fact, he looks like about a hundred dollars to me."

"Yeah, my hundred cos I saw him first," said Chick.

The greasy man, Lockjaw Lemmings himself, stood inside the swinging door and discharged a couple of shots before the troublemakers decided to move on. Relatives or no relatives, Lockjaw meant to do this one right. That bucket head, Chet, had gone and shot his own mother; therefore, a bounty had to be paid out.

The only thing bugging Lockjaw was that it looked like he might pay out the hundred dollars to a female. It wasn't that Lockjaw had much agin the feminine part of the species. It was just that it rankled that a woman was going to beat out all the other hombres looking for Chet Miller.

As soon as he pushed through the door of the trading post, Lockjaw was relieved to see two things: one—a man guarding the body, and the other...after he pulled the dead man's head back to make sure...the other—the unmistakable face of his polecat half-brother, Chet.

"That's him alright," Lockjaw said. He walked around the horse and held his hand out to Luther. "Mighty obliged to you for killing him."

"I didn't," said Luther.

Pearl came off the porch like a scalded dog. "Now you wait one damn minute. I killed that stinking sack of bones you see decoratin' that there horse. The bounty is mine."

Lockjaw turned to Luther. "That right, mister? Did she shoot him?"

Luther didn't say a word. Instead, he untied Chet and flipped him over for Lockjaw to see the knife wound. Then, still silent, he pointed at the handle of the knife on Pearl's belt.

"Law. If'n that don't beat all." He moved ahead of Pearl intending to go back into the trading post. "Hey, city boy, just dump that corpse up on the porch. Mind the door. I've got customers, you know."

"Come on, sugar tits, let me fetch that bounty for you," Lockjaw said to Pearl.

A roar sounded behind Pearl. She had just seconds to move out of the way before Luther jumped onto the back of Lockjaw Lemmings. He was pounding the daylights out of Lockjaw, who had no idea why he was being hit at all.

Lockjaw shucked Luther off his back and turned around to hit him back. Without backing off, Luther took up a pugilistic stance—fists in the air. Pearl just laughed, feeling flattered and flabbergasted all at the same time.

"What did you call the lady?" Luther demanded.

Lockjaw thought hard about his answer. Finally, he said, "Look mister, I must've made a mistake. I didn't know that the girl was yours. I'd never said, you know, what I did, if'n I'd knowed."

Luther looked over at Pearl. She was pulling Chet Miller up onto the porch by his feet, banging his poor head with every other step.

"She's not my girl, sir. Your remark was ungentlemanly, and I am a gentleman. As a matter of fact, I happen to be engaged to another. Perhaps you've heard of her? Miss Rita Odena Lay." Luther puffed out his chest with pride.

Lockjaw Lemmings looked first at Luther and then at Pearl. She shrugged. Then he burst out laughing. He slapped his thighs and threw back his head and whinnied as loud as any stallion.

"You take the cake, you two. You really do." He grinned like a possum rolling on the rotten body of a dead wolf. "Come on in and get your bounty. Hell, I'll throw in a shot of whiskey on that joke. I cain't remember when I've had such a good laugh."

Luther turned to Pearl. "What does he mean, Pearl?

Pearl bit her lip and sighed. "Damned if I know. I am powerfully thirsty. I think I'll get my stack of twenty-dollar gold pieces and take the man up on that whiskey."

Chapter Twenty-two

Range Detective Bill Puckett had plenty of time to ponder life's little idiosyncrasies, while he rode through the canyon on his way to Brown's Hole. He knew Pearl and the dandy had to be somewhere behind him. Still, they should have caught up by now. Maybe he had miscalculated, and the pair was gaining on him. If he holed up in one of the many Injun caves along the bluff, he should be able to pick off the man and take the girl captive.

He led the horses beside the river for a good drink. He did not want the three of them begging for water. Sitting it out a spell in one of the hollers seemed like a good idea, anyway. He had been riding since before daybreak, and the sun was beating down on him. He felt like an egg in a frying pan. Even though snow still covered the ground, and the air was cold, brilliant rays of sunshine heated his black overcoat to almost smoking.

He gathered the horses and angled onto his own pony, Pistol. He had won the chestnut mustang from an old Ute warrior in a knife throwing contest just outside of Denver. The horse was fast and loyal and seemed to ride forever. As Puckett rode along the river, he scanned the ridges and cliffs looking for an opening. Finally, he noticed a circular shadow about ten feet up one of the bluffs. He heeled the mustang and headed for it.

A little used trail led to the opening in the cliff, but the cave itself was spacious. A few small animal bones littered the floor; otherwise the interior was clean. He pulled all three horses inside and took up wait just inside the opening.

Not normally a curious man, Puckett spared little time wondering about the relationship between Pearl and the man. Instead, he planned how he would get Pecker's herd back to his ranch just outside of Vernal. He couldn't very well bring the cattle through the canyons, He pulled out a worn leather scroll and studied the area just west of Brown's Hole.

The map showed that once he cleared the hills surrounding Brown's Hole, he should be able to drive the cattle across the open grasslands west and then south to Pecker's ranch. He would have to rustle up at least a couple of hombres to help him get the herd back—hardcases, if he was smart. He needed to be careful. Sometimes those picked to protect a herd wound up wanting it for themselves. No point in getting the cattle to Utah only to have it stolen out from under him. He patted his six-guns and counted himself lucky he was fast on the draw. One dead cowpoke would convince any other would-be rustlers that he was a man who meant business and was not afraid to back it up.

The rock behind his back was flat and cool. Puckett took off his overcoat and leaned back against the wall to wait. He wasn't sleepy, but this was as good as time as any to rest. His Sharps rifle was beside him, so he sighted in on the spot he figured that Pearl would have to pass by. It shouldn't be long.

An hour passed before Puckett realized that he had been fooled. Irritation rose like bile in his throat. He knew the girl must have found some deer trail or other means of cutting through the canyons. The city man did not look the sort to have trail smarts. He would have to revise his plans.

Puckett saddled up his pony and led it and the two stallions down the side of the bluff. Once at the floor of the canyon, he mounted up and lit out beside the river again. It was entirely possible that Pearl had a good two hours on him, and the thought made him dig his heels in and goad his horse into a gallop. He did not want Pearl getting to Rita first. If anyone was going to kill that cheating, lying soiled dove, it was going to be him. He rode harder.

Not an hour out of Brown's Hole, his trail intersected with the one Pearl and Luther had taken. Puckett slowed when he saw the tracks, but something was off. There weren't two sets of tracks but three. He slid from his horse and carefully walked around the trail. Sure enough, there were three sets of tracks, and it was evident that they were traveling together.

He bent down to examine the hoof prints more closely. One horse was definitely Pearl's. The marks were lighter. It seemed that another horse was almost on top of her—probably riding just behind and carrying a man. The last set were also those of a man. The impression was deep.

He rubbed his chin and gazed into the valley that was Brown's Hole. Then he walked back to study the trail again. Pearl's hose was pulling the other horse. Puckett figured she had either taken someone prisoner, or the middle horse had been hauling a corpse. Judging by how close the horse was to hers, he figured it was the later.

Who had they killed? An Indian or an outlaw? Or was the man an outlaw himself who had captured Pearl and held the dandy hostage? Puckett pulled at an errant hair and ripped it free from his chin. He stuck it on his tongue and rolled it between his lips, considering the possibilities. There was certainly more to old man Pecker's daughter than he had thought.

He remembered seeing her across the river. She looked soft and womanly with her ample bosom and her firm rounded hips. He spit the coarse hair to the side. He smiled, but the smile did not reach his coal black, red-rimmed eyes. Puckett had not bedded a woman in a long time. Yes, Pearl might definitely give him a run for his money. He liked the idea of having a wildcat in his arms. She might fight him at first, but he would have fun taming her into submission. If Pearl somehow managed to get the cattle before he did, he would follow her and take them for his own. The cattle wouldn't be the only thing he would take.

Brown's Hole was just ahead, and Puckett hit the trail again. He was going to win this battle—just like he always won. No little girl and city boy were going to stop him. First, though, he had to find Rita, and when he caught up with her, there wouldn't be any taming. He planned to hurt her and then kill her. His face flushed red remembering how he had once begged Rita to love him. He had been a youngster then, but now he was a man. He wanted to hear her beg, beg for his mercy, beg for her life. He laughed thinking about it.

Bill Puckett rode into Brown's Hole and headed for Lockjaw's place. That greasy geezer was a gossip and a cheat, but his whiskey was cheap, and his tobacco was fresh. For a moment, Puckett wondered how the storekeeper was able to get the variety of goods he kept, but he really did not care enough to think on that for very long.

When Puckett got there ,there was a lone horse hitched to the rail in front of the trading post. He tied his three horses alongside it and went to brush through the batwings into the dark interior of the store. Something caught his eye on the porch by the door. He knelt to take another look. A faint impression of blood stained the rough wooden floor. He turned to glance behind him. Nothing. He felt the hairs on the back of his neck rise. He heard a click and whirled around.

The barrel of Lockjaw Lemmings' brand-new revolver, the Model 1875 Single Action Remington, touched the tip of Puckett's nose. Puckett didn't move a muscle. Lockjaw stroked the trigger with his index finger and grinned like an evil monkey.

"What's it going to be, mister? Are you coming in to buy something, or are you standing outside my trading post figuring to do something else?"

Puckett went to remove his hat. Lockjaw's thumb eased back on the hammer. Both men locked eyes. Then Lockjaw started laughing.

"Come on in, you old sidewinder, and have a drink on me."

"Smells like you already had a few," said Puckett.

"That's highly likely." Lockjaw spied the two horses tied up beside the mustang. "Them horses look mighty familiar. They the Lay brothers?"

"They could be."

"Must be the day for killing and collecting," Lockjaw said.

"What do you mean by that?"

"Hell, come into the shade, and let's have a sip. Then I'll tell you all about it."

They walked into the trading post and headed for the bar. Lockjaw waved Puckett to a stool. He poured them both a drink. It went down like liquid fire. He poured another shot.

"You'll never guess who I met today," Lockjaw said.

Puckett studied his drink, letting his throat recover from the first hit of rock gut. "I don't like to guess. Who?" He tossed back his drink.

"Your old girlfriend's new boyfriend."

Puckett choked on his drink and then grabbed Lockjaw's throat.

"Who?" He sputtered and coughed, until tears flew from his eyes. Still Puckett maintained his grip on the storekeeper's throat.

"Rita's fiancé. Some wet-behind-the-ears dentist. Came up here all the way from Boston. Said that she was his darling." He tried to push Puckett's hand away, but Puckett would not let go. It was almost as though he was choking Rita. Lockjaw Lemmings reached for the empty whiskey bottle on the counter and slammed it down on Puckett's head.

Bill Puckett's head hit the pine counter with a pop. Then he fell face forward over the bar.

"Son of a dad-burned biscuit eater. Attack a man in his own establishment." He shoved Puckett off the bar onto the floor. "What would his mama say?"

Lockjaw shook his head and then wiped down the counter.

Chapter Twenty-three

After Pearl and Luther left the trading post, they headed over to the Fuller House. Maggie Fuller was a decent cook and a genuinely nice woman. As a youngster, she had come to Brown's Hole with a wily outlaw named Harvey Fuller. He had been a card shark and a thief, and no one had ever figured out what Maggie saw in him. Still, he was long dead and gone, and Maggie had stayed on in the two-story house he had built for them. She had turned the place into a hotel of sorts, and many a desperado had eaten his last meal there.

A hand-painted sign on the porch stated Maggie's rules: No cussing, spitting, or shooting. Two big red-boned hounds snoozed on either end of the porch. They looked benign, but if anyone had dared attack their mistress, they would have taken them apart. Maggie knew that, of course, but she backed up their protection with a little of her own. Under her apron was a low-slung holster complete with a pair of Smith and Wesson pistols.

Even though she wasn't quick on the draw, Maggie was lucky. No man west of the Mississippi had mauled or raped her; and if she had anything to say about it, they never would.

Pearl handed Luther Belle's reins and sauntered up to the open doorway and called out, "Miss Maggie, you've got two customers. We need some grub and a place to wash up."

Wiping flour-covered hands on her apron, Maggie appeared at the door. She looked first at Pearl and then at Luther who was still in the yard trying to tie up the horses. Belle was after his ear again, and Luther was dodging and weaving trying to avoid losing it to the horse.

"He with you?" Maggie asked.

Pearl looked back at Luther. He was slapping away at Belle's nose. Finally, the mare knocked him to the ground. Luther scooted on his backside across the muddy yard.

She turned to Maggie. "Sort of."

"Pearl, Pearl. Relieve me of this animal. Call off your horse!"

Pearl ignored him. Instead, she asked Maggie, "Smells like you're cooking up something mighty wonderful in there. Are you open for business? We need a hot meal and a bath."

They glanced at Belle rolling Luther through the mud.

"He really needs the bath. And his suit could use a brushing down," Pearl said.

"I only got one spare room." Maggie's lips tightened. "You two don't look married to me."

"Hell..." Pearl glanced at the sign and coughed. "Heck no, we aint' married, and we ain't sharing no bed either." She jerked her thumb Luther's way. "He's engaged. We met up on the trail, and now we's here. He wants to hitch up with his fiancée."

Luther had managed to elude Belle. He stumbled up the steps and onto the porch beside Pearl. "Pearl's entirely correct, madam. I've come a long way to see my darling fiancée. Miss Rita Odena Lay."

Maggie looked startled. She snickered. "Is that so? Rita Lay, you said?" She glanced at Pearl, who was trying her best to look innocent. "Do tell?" Maggie moved aside to let her visitors in the house. "Come on back to the kitchen. I can't wait to hear about this."

When they entered the front hallway of the ranch house, Maggie directed Luther to the stairs. "There's a pitcher of water and some towels upstairs. You can take a proper bath later, if'n you a mind to. In the meantime, you need to get some of that mud off you."

The rest of the hallway cut down the middle of the house and ended at the kitchen. It was a large, cheerful room with a wood cookstove and two large pine tables. Pearl perched at the table nearest the stove and took off her overcoat. The room was warm and smelled of biscuits and gravy.

"I've just cooked up some liver and onions with gravy, if you'd like some," said Maggie.

Pearl was practically drooling. "Miss Maggie, I think I've died and gone to Heaven."

"Well, you shouldn't." Maggie banged a giant wooden ladle on the table in front of Pearl. "What are you thinking letting a good-looking, single man like that go to some hog-faced bitch like Rita Lay?" She turned back to her cooking. "I almost swallowed my tongue when I heard what he said."

"So, she's here then?" Pearl asked.

"Oh, she's in Brown's Hole all right. She and those two weasels she claims as brothers rode in here first part of last week. The twins left, though. Supposed to have gone back down to Vernal, before picking up some man friend of Rita's. She had a herd of cattle and was hiring ranch hands left and right. Ain't much pickings here, though, for hands. Most of the ones she hired are either outlaws or drifters. She'll be lucky to have half her herd in a week."

"That ain't her herd. They's my pa's," Pearl said flatly.

For the first time, Maggie showed Pearl true sympathy. "Oh dear. I'm sorry. What are you going to do?"

Pearl wiped away a tear of self-pity and straightened her spine. "I'm going after her and take back what's mine."

"That might not be so simple, dear. Them some bad hombres working for Rita." Maggie spooned some of the liver and gravy onto a plate for Pearl. "What about him? He don't know. Does he?" She leaned into look in Pearl's eyes. "Why haven't you told him?"

"I tried, but he don't listen."

"Most men never do, dear."

Pearl did not say a word. She didn't have to. Miss Maggie had seen more than one girl hooked up with the wrong man, and she was sorry to see it here. Pearl was going to get hurt, and there was nothing she could do about it. Still...

The aroma of the breakfast overcame Pearl, and she dig into the delicious meal. The gravy was silk smooth, and the combination of liver and onions was as fortifying as it was tasty. Pearl could feel her belly growing warmer and her resolve growing firmer with each bite.

"I will get my cattle back," Pearl said. "And I am going to make that Rita pay. I just don't want to hurt Third Luther." She shook her head.

"Hurt him? Darling, you'd be saving that poor bastard from a fate worse than death." Maggie slapped the table with her hand. "Law, you should see her. She's been gallivanting around dressed up in a white wedding gown for the past three days. Ain't much telling what she smells like by now. She's stuffed so tight in that contraption; if'n she farts, she'll bust a gusset."

"She still fat?"

"Fatter than a pig. How in God's name did he get hooked up with her?"

"Pony express," said Pearl.

"Oh, one of those."

They looked sheepishly toward the door. Luther was coming down the hall, his boots echoing on the wood floors. Pearl went back to her eating, while Miss Maggie busied herself at the stove. Both women looked as innocent as angels. Luther smiled at the heart-warming domestic scene.

"The mouthwatering aroma literally drew me down the stairs," he said.

Maggie laughed and broke open a couple of her steaming hot biscuits, and then she covered them with gravy and liver and onions. When she handed the plate to Luther, he grabbed it with both hands. He looked as delighted as a little child and tucked into his meal with as much gusto.

Pearl looked over at Luther happily eating his plate of food and wished she had put that smile on his face. Suddenly, she felt drained. Soon, she and Luther would go their separate ways. Once she captured Rita and took back her pa's cattle, there would be no need for them to stay together. He might even hate her for destroying his dream. Depression settled over Pearl's heart like a shroud.

Maggie looked over at Pearl and seemed to read her mind. She rounded the table in seconds, took Pearl by the arm, and led her away from Luther. Pearl could not help the rush of feelings, and she struggled not to cry, until they were out of the room.

"Hey," Luther called, "what's the matter? Do you need my help?" He had never known Pearl to look weak like that.

"She's just tired. Probably a female thing," Maggie called back. To Pearl she said, "Men folk never want an explanation of female things. I'm not sure what comes to mind when a woman says that, but it must be mighty scary to them."

Pearl couldn't help but laugh a little. "I don't know what happened to me," she said as they climbed the stairs. "I started thinking about him with Rita..."

"You was thinking too much," Maggie said. "You got to just let things come to pass." She opened the door to a cozy little bedroom. Luther's jacket hung on a peg by the door. Pearl touched the arm of the jacket and sighed, but she didn't have time to feel sorry for herself. In quick time, Maggie helped her undress and tucked her into bed like a baby.

"I'll wash these clothes of yours. They will be dry in no time."

"I've got to catch Rita," Pearl said. Her eyes started to close.

"You can catch that old soiled dove, when you've got more strength. She's too fat to run too far in that get-up she's wearing."

Pearl laughed sleepily and snuggled deep into the feather mattress. "I guess a few minutes couldn't hurt." She was snoring in seconds.

Maggie looked at the cloud of black hair surrounding Pearl's sweet face. She could not help but compare it to the made-up mask of that tramp Rita. Still, Maggie knew how things were between men and women. Luther might be the sort to want a woman with more experience. Rita certainly had that going for her.

Yep, things were about to get mighty interesting around Brown's Hole. Maggie gathered up Pearl's clothes and trudged down the stairs to wash them up. Upstairs, Pearl dreamed of a handsome man and a hung hussy.

Chapter Twenty-four

After Luther finished his breakfast, he looked around for his jacket. He was itching to explore Brown's Hole and find his beloved Rita. Not knowing that the valley was nearly fifty miles long and named for Baptiste Brown, a man who quit Hudson Bay in the early 1800's and settled with his wife in the basin; Luther assumed it would be relatively easy to find Rita and her mythical ranch. Little did he know that Rita was as hot on his trail as he was on hers.

Maggie was hanging out Pearl's clothes on a length of twine that stretched from one post of the back porch to the other, when Luther wandered out the back door. The wind was whipping up something fierce. Maggie figured that the garments would be dry within a couple of hours. Luther stood quietly in the doorway watching her work.

"Miss Maggie, I don't know how to thank you for taking care of us like this. Why, such hospitality is beyond my experience. Folks in Boston are friendly enough, to be sure, but out here people seem to go out of their way to help one another."

"You ain't met many people. Have you, son?" Maggie harrumphed. "Who you basing all this so-called hospitality on? Me?"

"No, madam...well, yes, in part. But look at Pearl. She rescued me and saved my life more than once on this journey to my darling Rita, and Mr. Lemmings was so friendly and offered us a drink at his trading establishment."

"Most likely you're right about Pearl. She is a kind soul, and I try to provide good food and rest for travelers through these parts. But, that's how I make my living." She smiled. The reminder was there. Miss Maggie's hospitality wasn't the free kind. "And old Lockjaw is a troublemaker and a gossip. If'n I didn't know better, I'd figure that right at this very moment he's a stirring up a brew of mischief as we speak. So, son, there's some nice people in these parts for sure. Ain't any of us saints."

Luther nodded. He walked to the edge of the porch and looked out over the countryside. Coming out West had exceeded his every expectation. He was sure that once he met his wife to be, everything would be even better. He could join her in running her ranch. Even though he knew next to nothing about cattle, Luther was certain that he could learn and succeed.

He turned to Maggie. "Do you know where I left my jacket? I cannot seem to find it. I'm ready to meet my future wife. Once I say my goodbyes to Pearl, I'll be on my way. I'm sure that Rita is beginning to worry about me by now. The blizzard has made me days late, and it's been upsetting though unavoidable. I have always prided myself on being punctual."

Maggie's eye held a twinkle. "Well, Luther, that's a good quality to be sure." Maggie might have accused Lockjaw Lemmings of stirring up trouble, but she wasn't above a little mischief-making of her own. "I just remembered where I saw that jacket of yours. It was in the bedroom upstairs."

"Thanks, Miss Maggie. I'll just run and fetch it."

"Now don't..." She stopped. She had almost told him not to bother Pearl, but she hoped the opposite would be true.

"Madam?" he asked, but Maggie had hurried off after a piece of laundry the wind had whisked away. She had no desire to see him wed to a hog's wart like Rita Lay. If he managed to discover how he really felt about Pearl, then all the better. She decided to hold her tongue and see what happened.

The foot of the stairway was to the right of the front door. Luther walked up the hallway through the middle of the house, wondering how such a nice lady like Miss Maggie could live alone in a valley known for harboring outlaws and cattle rustlers. The more he thought about it, this seemed an odd location for Rita's ranch. She had written that she had two brothers who worked the cattle with her. He nodded, understanding. Rita had protection. What about Miss Maggie? Who protected her?

As he started up the stairs, another question gave him pause. Who would protect Pearl? Pearl had said that she was retrieving her father's cattle, but she had never said from whom. What if it was from an evil desperado? Didn't he owe Pearl his protection?

The more he thought about Pearl—alone and at the mercy of murdering cattle rustlers—the more Luther realized his inability to protect her. This was not Boston or London. This was the Wild West, just like in the dime store novels, replete with gun-toting killers, Indians, and outlaws. Luther knew he was ill-equipped to handle the sort of trouble a man came up against in the West.

The door to the spare bedroom was closed tightly. Carefully, Luther eased it open so as not to wake Pearl. He need not have bothered. Pearl had been exhausted, and nothing short of a complete calamity would wake her now.

Luther stood for a moment just looking at her face. The blush of her cheeks was echoed in her full red lips. Her porcelain skin gleamed against the hand-sewn quilt pulled tightly to her chin. At that moment, Luther saw how beautiful Pearl really was. Something in his chest grew tight. Painful.

He thought about the night in the cave, when she had snuggled close to his chest, warming his body with her own. Saving his life, yet again. The way he had felt the next morning, as she lay full and womanly in his arms. For just an instant, he wanted to recapture that feeling. He wanted to hold her and have her body mold itself to his.

Luther moved closer to the bed. What was he doing? He stepped back. His eyes never left her face. It was as though he was drawn to her. The next thing he knew, he had forgotten all about his jacket. He lay down on the bed beside her but on top of the quilt. His arms were held stiffly at his sides, and it was not until Pearl turned and threw her arm around him that he relaxed.

In sleep, she instinctively turned to him. Luther did not want to ponder the implications of that. She was loud and strong and often too damn sure of herself for her own good, but Luther admired Pearl more than he thought prudent to let her know. He pulled her head against his chest and lay still, enjoying the smell of her hair and the feel of her arm wrapped tightly around him.

The soft feather bed enveloped them, warming them, urging Luther to sleep. They were both tuckered out and filled to the brim with Miss Maggie's good cooking. Luther's eyes closed. In sleep, he turned and drew Pearl closer. His arms folded around her back, and he rested his chin in her hair. Luther sighed while Pearl gently snored.

An hour passed. The wind blew every speck of moisture from Pearl's clothes hanging on the make-shift clothesline on Miss Maggie's back porch. Side by side, they swung back and forth—her blouse, the long-skirt, a pair of trousers, and her unmentionables. Outside, Miss Maggie looked up at the window of her spare bedroom and smiled. Luther and Pearl had been up there for a long time. She pulled Pearl's clothes off the twine clothesline and took them in the house to warm by the stove.

Even though they were dry, no one alive would want to put on underwear that had hung out in almost freezing weather. The skirt would need a good ironing to keep it from hanging stiff. She had just put the flat iron on the stovetop, when she heard a loud thump on the front porch followed closely by a scream and then a torrent of cursing. Maggie's hounds started bawling.

Pearl's skirt was tossed onto a chair. Miss Maggie shoved one hand under her apron, grabbing for her pistol as she ran like hell down the hallway toward the front of her house.

The gun leapt into her right hand. She yanked it clear of her apron just in time to see who the intruder was. Or rather what it was.

Belle had pulled free of her hitch and was clomping around the porch trying to bite the veil off the head of a screaming, cussing, hellion of a bride. The bride was hanging onto her headpiece and hollering like a cat in heat surrounded by a clowder of tom cats. Miss Maggie pulled the hammer back on her gun in case Belle got hurt in the fight, but it looked to her like the mare had a good chance of winning.

Finally, Miss Maggie decided the ruckus had gone on long enough. She sighted in on the bride's foot and tried her best to shoot it. The pistol roared. Its smoke hadn't cleared, when Miss Maggie said her adieus.

"Good-bye, Rita. You ain't wanted here."

Chapter Twenty-five

After Rita had sent her brothers to Vernal for more supplies and then on to fetch Luther, she had begun preparations for their wedding. A few days later, she had worried that sending the evil, hard-headed duo after Luther had been a mistake. Those two almost killed each other on a daily basis. They were constantly arguing and shooting off their mouths *and* guns. For all she knew, they could have shot Luther and left him to die in some canyon. So, when Rita heard from the notorious gossip, Lockjaw Lemmings, that not only was Luther in town, but he was accompanied by a female bounty hunter name of Pearl Hawthorne, she was mad enough to pop her corset.

Rita had figured out for herself where her good-lucking fiancé had gone for a hot meal. There was only one decent place in Brown's Hole—the Fuller house. Maggie Fuller was the best cook for a hundred miles, and Rita had known without being told that Lockjaw would send the pair to Miss Maggie's for grub.

What she did not know was that Bill Puckett was also in the valley. Puckett had been hiding under the counter the entire time Rita had been in the trading post. His gun had been cocked and pointed at Lockjaw Lemmings' family jewels. That alone had been ample incentive for Lockjaw to keep his silence. Puckett needed a diversion, so he could round up the stolen cattle and then finish off Rustlin' Rita. Her fiancé with another woman was a sure-fire distraction for a woman in heat.

Oblivious to the upcoming commotion, Luther and Pearl slept on. During the afternoon, the quilt shifted. Pearl's left breast peeked out from under the covers. Luther's fingers had curled underneath its softness. Pearl's lips were just touching the side of Luther's throat. All in all, the scene was a cozy one...one that proved to be a mite too intimate in just a matter of minutes.

"Lu-ther!" Rita screamed. She yanked her veil free from Belle's big golden choppers, threw back her head and screamed at Maggie. "You damn near shot my foot off, you bitch."

"Call me that one more time, and I won't miss again. You'll walk with a limp for the rest of your worthless life," said Maggie. She pulled the other pistol from her holster. "You want to dance, Rita? I got the music."

"Get out of my way, Maggie. He's mine, and I aim to take him with me." Rita looked down with pride at her wedding dress. She did not notice that it was two sizes too tight or that its hem was soiled. She only saw her bulging bosom and the piles and piles of white lace sewn to its skirt.

"This is my house, and ain't no one going in what I don't say so," said Maggie.

Maggie and Rita stood face to face, staring into one another's eyes. Then, out of the blue, Rita dodged to her left and then hooked Maggie's chin with a mean right. She cold cocked Maggie, who staggered back just a second, crossed her eyes, and went down. Rita looked down at her opponent. Maggie was laid flat out, but her eyes were still twitching.

Rita didn't have much time. When Maggie came to, she would unload those Smith and Wessons into Rita's backside and nothing would stop her. Grabbing her lace skirt, Rita vaulted over Maggie's body and burst through the front door into the house. She looked first one way and then the other, and then she looked up the stairs. Her eyes narrowed.

Luther was upstairs, and something told her that Pearl was up there with him. The thought of Pearl alone with Luther had Rita charging up the stairs. At the top of the stairway, the stairs made a hard left to the landing. She careened off the side-rail and slammed into the wall. Rita did not feel a thing. Her man, her Luther, was up there somewhere.

The door to the little bedroom stood ajar. Rita could hear snores coming from the room. Two snores. With a howl, she yanked up the hem of her dress and slammed her foot into the door, screaming at the top of her lungs.

"Where is he? Where is my fiancé?"

Luther jumped up in the bed. Startled, Pearl clung to him. Her full creamy breasts spilled out over the top of the quilt. They looked at one another and screamed.

The scene was more than Rita could stomach. She looked wildly around the room for a weapon. Pearl's Winchester was propped against the footboard of the bed. Rita grabbed for the gun and worked the lever, intending to blow Pearl's brains out right then and there.

"Madam, don't!" shouted Luther.

Pearl searched under her pillow for her Derringer. It was caught in the pillowcase. Her fingers frantically worked to free her little gun. Rita was coming closer and closer. Finally, Pearl managed to free the gun. She drew the tiny revolver, holding it eye-level with Rita.

"I'll be damned if you shoot me with my own rifle," screamed Pearl. She thumbed the hammer, but Luther grabbed her arm. The shot went wild.

"Then you'll be damned. Because if'n I ain't mistaken, I'm about to shoot you right now," said Rita.

Pearl leaped across Luther and over the bedrail. She was naked as a jaybird except for her boots. She fired at Rita again, hitting her in the arm. Blood spurted onto the wedding dress. Rita went wild. She was pumping the rifle's lever, shooting blindly, emptying shells on the bedroom rug, but not hitting Pearl who dived to the floor between Rita and the bed. Then Pearl jumped to her feet, running hell for leather down the stairs.

Luther had rolled out of the way and was cowering under the bed.

"You be careful, darling," yelled Rita. "I don't want no corpse for a groom."

"Don't worry, you old fat fish-face. Now that he's seen you, he probably ain't going to marry you anyway," Pearl hollered as she ran.

Pearl brushed by Maggie, who had pulled the hammer on both pistols and was headed up the stairs.

"Sorry for the trouble, Miss Maggie. I'll settle up with you in a few days." Pearl ran for the front door.

"Pearl, your clothes are in the kitchen," yelled Maggie shooting her pistols up the stairway. "Light out the back way. I'll cover those two upstairs."

Pearl's boots scraped a line on the wood floorboards, as she slid to a halt, then she whirled around and sprinted for the kitchen. She grabbed her underwear and the rest of her clothes and took off around the house. Buck naked and freezing, Pearl leaped onto Belle's back, pulling the reins into her hands. The mare reared back, whinnying with excitement. From the upstairs window, Miss Maggie tossed Pearl's Winchester down to her. With her other hand, Maggie kept a revolver trained on Rita Lay.

"Get going, Pearl," Maggie yelled. To Rita, she said, "You'll be a lucky ducky, if'n I don't blow your foolish head off. What the hell do you mean bushwhacking me and then shooting up my house? I ought to ventilate you just for the sport of it."

Luther crawled out from under the bed. With his dignity tattered but not totally stolen, he got to his feet and smoothed down his suit. He looked at Rita, and then, being the gentleman he was, he held out his hand.

"Madam, I don't think we've been introduced."

Rita looked at Maggie and smiled like they were best friends. "Would you look at that?" She shook her head in amazement. "Ain't he grand? Ain't he just grand?"

Miss Maggie started to chuckle. "He's something else, but the sharpest rock in the box, he ain't." She pushed her six guns back into their holster and took first Rita's hand and then Luther's in hers. She placed their hands together. Then she said, "Miss Rita Odena Lay, may I introduce you to Luther...?"

"Luther Van Buren the third," said Luther.

Tears of joy in her eyes, Rita nodded.

"And Luther, may I introduce you to your fiancée, Miss Rita Lay better known around these parts as Rustlin' Rita."

Luther looked at Rita. The shock of the shoot-out finally wore off. He shook his head, trying to understand what Miss Maggie had just said. This was Rita? His darling Rita?

"Did you say Rustlin' Rita?" he asked hoarsely.

"Now just a minute," Rita said, but Miss Maggie cut her off.

"I sure as hell did. Meet your fiancée. The one who stole Pearl's cattle."

Luther's face turned a funny yellow color. His vision blurred. He fainted.

Chapter Twenty-six

Any qualms Pearl might have had about riding off and leaving Luther behind had ended when he crawled under the bed. One minute he had been holding her breast, and the next he was hiding while his darling, Rustlin' Rita tried to fill her full of lead. At least, she had got one good shot off, even if it hadn't killed Rita. Better than that belly-crawler had managed. It was one thing to be lousy with a gun and another to be gun shy.

Pearl was freezing her ass off. Literally. She needed somewhere to hole up and get her britches on. Her butt was turning blue and chill bumps covered her skin. She felt like a plucked chicken. The wind was so cold. It seemed like it was cutting streaks across her body. She turned her horse back toward Lockjaw's trading post. Her heels dug into Belle's side, and the mare needed no further encouragement. As ripe with pent-up emotion as her mistress, Belle galloped hard and fast.

Not far from Lockjaw's place, she galloped past another rider that was moving faster than a jackrabbit with its tail on fire. It was Range Detective Bill Puckett. When he saw Pearl, naked with her hair flying wild, he involuntarily pulled hard on the reins of his mustang. Pistol, his horse, stopped so suddenly that Puckett slid sideways off his saddle. He landed with one foot on the ground and the other caught in the stirrup. As Pistol pranced around, Puckett did a one-legged dance beside him.

Even though she could feel Puckett's eyes on her butt, Pearl stood high in the saddle urging her horse to go faster. She recognized Puckett, but at that moment, she didn't care if he got to the cattle first. Some things had to take priority even over her pa's cattle. One of those things had to be getting dressed. The cold wind was stinging her body from head to toe.

When Pearl burst through the batwings of the trading post, Lockjaw Lemmings lost all ability to speak. For once, the old gossip was speechless. A naked woman in the trading post... His eyes almost burst right out of their sockets. Pearl couldn't help but notice that Lockjaw's tongue was hanging out of his mouth.

Pearl headed for the stove in the middle of the store. She was so cold she felt like she would never catch her breath. She wrapped her arms tightly around herself, coughing and choking for air. The wind had parched her throat, until it had almost closed shut. She turned back and forth in front of the stove trying to get warm. Her hands were numb from holding the reins, and she rubbed and slapped her arms and legs, trying to get some blood flowing.

"Not one word, Lockjaw, or I'll shoot you dead right here in your own establishment. I swear to God I will," she said, as she left the heater and stomped to the back of the store. She saw the tall counter at the bar. In one swift movement, she flipped the Winchester, cocking it using only one hand. In spite of his amazement at Pearl's nudity, Lockjaw was almost as impressed by her dexterity. His hands went up, and he angled out from behind the counter. He could not quit staring at her.

"Turn around, you polecat," Pearl said.

Lockjaw spun around. "I just want to say, Miss Pearl, that you are one fine-looking woman. I'd of never guessed how..." Lockjaw thought it best to stop right there.

Pearl wasn't easily put off. "Never of guessed what?" She hopped around the counter and tried pulling her britches over her boots. They wouldn't go. Disgusted, she kicked her boots off and tried again. "I asked you a question, Lockjaw."

Lockjaw was thinking of an answer because he had been about to mention the size of her bosom. He considered lying, but he couldn't think of a good one to save his life."

"Well, Pearl, I was just going to say that you have some mighty purty tits." He heard a gun click and hurried to finish his explanation. "I don't mean no disrespect with that comment, either. It's just that I ain't hardly ever seen a woman...you know, a woman all naked and everything."

"That's probably true. I'll give you that," Pearl said. "But if'n I hear one word about this from anyone, I'll be the very last naked woman you see. Mark my words on that one."

Lockjaw made the sign of the cross and kissed his fingers. "I swear on my mother's grave that I'll never tell a soul."

Pearl fired the Winchester over his head, causing chunks of clay to fall from the ceiling. "Your mother ain't dead. She lives in Denver"

"Hell, Pearl, she's bound to die someday."

Pearl had to concede that what Lockjaw said made sense. She knew that once she was gone, Lockjaw would tell the next customer through the batwings that he had seen Pearl Hawthorne, old man Pecker's daughter, naked. She just hoped that he wouldn't get too fancy with the details.

Once she was dressed, Pearl tucked the Derringer back into her wool vest and went back to the fire to warm up a bit more. She combed her fingers through her hair. It was a tangled mess. Without saying a word, Lockjaw scurried over to a shelf and pulled down a hairbrush and took it over to her. He smiled like a fool in love, and in truth he was. Seeing Pearl naked had tripped something in Lockjaw's heart, and Pearl hated to see it.

She blushed and took the brush. "Thank-ee, Lockjaw. That was nice of you."

His eyes grew wider. He grinned, showing every tooth in his head—though there weren't too many of them.

"Quit looking at me like that, or I'll be forced to blow your brains out," Pearl said.

But Lockjaw Lemmings was smitten. He had seen Pearl in all her naked glory, and he would never forget it. Even dressed, she was beautiful, but he could still imagine her gleaming naked body. He kept staring at her.

Pearl shuddered. Looking at Lockjaw reminded her of a day back in the orphanage when she was a little girl. A mouse had run into the kitchen, and the sister in charge of the house had let in the nunnery cat. The cat was black and white and had grown rather fat. Still, Pearl could still see the face of the mouse—the way it looked when the cat backed it into a corner. The horrid fascination of the mouse's face just before the cat pounced and gobbled it up. Lockjaw had that same look. Pearl realized that she couldn't be the cat. She couldn't shoot Lockjaw. He was just a poor stupid mouse of a man.

"Miss Pearl, would you like a drop of whiskey to help thaw out your bones. If'n you don't mind my saying so, you still look a little blue about the gills."

Whiskey sounded good to Pearl, but she wished she had her tonic. "Lockjaw, you wouldn't have some of old Percival's Merciful, would you? I feel a cold coming on strong, and I ain't got any more tonic."

Lockjaw ran to fetch a tonic. "No ma'am, I ain't got Old Percy's, but what I do got is some tongue oil that will grow hair on your chest. It's called Miss Petunia's Potion and Elixir. Not that you need hair on your chest. No, ma'am, you don't. Not with them tits. I mean, uh, what I mean is...?

"Just bring it here. My innards are as cold as my ass, Lockjaw. My teeth won't stop chattering. I'm afraid the damn things are going to break off from hitting each other so hard."

For the life of her, Pearl couldn't seem to warm up. When Lockjaw handed her the flat, little bottle of elixir, Pearl uncorked it and swallowed half the contents in one gulp. Then her eyes almost bulged right out of her head. Nothing could have prepared her for the burst of fire that lit in her stomach and traveled down every nerve ending in her body. If her hair had not already been brushed out, it would have straightened out of its own accord.

"Whoooo-eee! Hot damn!" yelled Pearl. "You son of a biscuit eater."

Pearl's nostrils flared trying to suck in more air. From her guts to her ear lobes, she felt like lightning bolts were traveling through her body. Her eyes dilated, and then she smiled. It was a crazy, dare the devil, shake hands with St. Peter kind of smile, and it almost scared the boots plum off Lockjaw Lemmings.

She turned to look at him, and then she did the wildest thing of all. Pearl ran over to Lockjaw and planted the biggest, wettest kiss he had ever had laid on him. All the desire and anger in her came out in that one kiss. Lockjaw staggered back against the wood stove. He grabbed the stovepipe to steady himself and ended up knocking the pipe clean out of the stove. Soot and smoke quickly filled the trading post, and just before the flames leapt out of the stove's belly, Pearl heard Lockjaw shout, "I love you, Miss Pearl. I love you with all my heart."

Pearl ran for the front door. She looked back at Lockjaw standing there, tar-faced and grinning. "Hey, Lockjaw, what about that buckskin of Chet's that I brought in?"

"Take him. He's yours."

"Thanks. Can you keep him for me a little while? I'll be back to get him and some supplies. I promise," Pearl said.

Lockjaw just kept on grinning and nodding like a fool.

"You might ought to put out that fire, Lockjaw. before you burn up the whole damn place."

At a run, Pearl yanked her skirt up and jumped for Belle's saddle. She thrust her Winchester in the scabbard and pulled the mare around heading after Bill Puckett. Sure, he had a good lead on her, but she knew just where he was headed. He was after the cattle, but Pearl had the better claim. She wasn't about to let that varmint Puckett get what was hers. When she finished with him and had her cattle, then she planned on taking care of Rustlin" Rita.

Fired up on Miss Petunia's elixir, which was almost like drinking pure alcohol, Pearl felt like she could whoop any man and tame any beast. She pulled the little Derringer from her vest and fired it into the air. Then she lit out after Puckett, the fastest gunslinger in Brown's Hole.

Chapter Twenty-seven

Luther was out—stone cold on the bedroom floor. Miss Maggie and Rita knelt beside him, holding his hands and waiting for him to wake up. Out of the corner of her eye, Rita glanced at Miss Maggie. Maggie had let Pearl get clean away, and she wasn't about to forget it. Besides, there would have been plenty of time for Luther to find out about the cattle. Now was not the time. Especially, since Rita had gone to so much trouble to steal them, so Luther would think she was a rich cattle woman.

The ruse had worked, and Luther was in Brown's Hole. If Rita had her way, they would be married within the hour. If that meant getting rid of Miss Maggie and her interfering ways, then so be it.

"Luther, can you hear me?" Maggie asked. She leaned down to listen to his heart. She was facing away from Rita, and that was all the chance Rustlin' Rita needed.

"Yes, darling, can you hear us? Are you awake, honey lamb?" Silently, she looked around the room. Luther's holster was draped over the bedpost. "Baby lamb, it's me. Your fiancée." She moved to grab one of the Colts from the holster.

Too late, Maggie noticed Rita reaching over her head. Wham! Rita turned the gun on its side and slammed it against Maggie's head. With a grunt, Maggie fell against Luther, and Rita brushed her off Luther's chest as though she was no more than a pesky fly.

Rita grabbed the bedpost and hauled herself up. The wedding dress was more bulky than heavy. Still, she didn't need to be wallowing around on the floor in it. For a moment, Rita caught a glimpse of herself in the dresser mirror. Preening like a fat little bird seeing its reflection in a puddle of water, Rita pranced around in front of the mirror. She thought the wedding dress was beautiful. Except for a few spots of dirt and some splatters of blood where Pearl's shot had grazed her arm, the dress was remarkably clean.

Without giving him a thought, Rita stepped over Luther and headed for a water pitcher and basin on the dresser. She poured a little water in the basin and commenced to wash up her arms and dab at the spots on her dress. The wound stung a little, but it was only a flesh wound— really more of a burn. The bullet had not penetrated the skin. The very idea of Pearl shooting her had Rita right pissed off.

She had never liked Pearl Hawthorne as a kid, and she sure as hell didn't like her now. She looked down at the bloody water and took the basin over to the open window, where she pitched it down the side of the house. Then she poured some more of the water into the bowl and tossed it square on Luther's face.

"Time for a wedding, darling Luther," she said.

Luther woke straight up and sat to one side, trying to get his senses back together. Rita reached down and grabbed his hand. She gazed into his face, and for the first time he really looked at hers. This was his beautiful fiancée? He groped in his vest pocket for the photograph that he kept next to his heart.

Rita's eyes narrowed when she saw him looking first at the worn pictures and then at her. His eyes kept going back and forth. Rita was getting madder and madder.

"Who is this?" Luther asked.

"Who the hell you think it is?" Rita tried to mimic the picture's smile.

It didn't work. She bore only a slight resemblance to her cousin, the real subject of the photograph.

"Okay, so it ain't me, "she said. "But she is my cousin, and more than one person has said we's look alikes."

Without being offensive, Luther could find nothing to say in reply. He sat staring up at his bride to be in all her glory. Like the woman in the picture, she did have blond hair, but that was the only similarity that he could see. Rita was almost six feet tall and was as broad as a barn. She was rough—windblown ruddy cheeks, hard callused hands, and the stance of a cowpoke.

In other circumstances, he would have pitied her. As it was, she was holding his gun, and after the shoot-out with Pearl, he had no doubt she would use it. He held his hand up to her.

"Madam, would you mind helping me to my feet?"

Rita almost swooned at his accent. She found it so cultured and romantic. "I would be delighted," she said.

What her coquettish skills lacked in deportment, they made up for in sincerity. Rita wanted to be desirable, and she thought that by trying hard enough she would be. Luther almost felt sorry for her, but not sorry enough to marry her.

"Why did you feel you had to trick me into coming out here?" He held up the picture. "This is clearly not you, and you don't have any cattle."

"Now you hang on just one damn minute. That is my cousin, and I do so have cattle. I stole them cattle fair and square. They don't call me Rustlin' Rita for nuthin'. I've been relieving folks of their livestock for nigh on five years now, and I ain't went to jail for it once. Them is my cattle, Luther."

"But...but they are Pearl's cattle!"

"Well, no they ain't hers, either. They's really her pa's, and that old sawed-off bastard is meaner than ten rattlesnakes. Getting them cattle back ain't going to make him love Pearl, if'n he don't love her already. And he don't, by the way."

"I'm sure we could debate this all day, Miss Lay," said Luther.

The 'Miss Lay' told Rita all she needed to know. Luther was already trying to get out of marrying her. That just wasn't going to happen. They were getting married within the hour, if she had any say in the matter. She did not care if she had to hog-tie him to get him to the alter.

For once, Luther was able to read the look on a woman's face and tell exactly what she was thinking. Without so much as a polite by your leave, he grabbed for his holster, turned on his heel, and skedaddled the hell out of the Fuller House. He was worried about Miss Maggie, but there wasn't anything he could do for her. She would come to in a bit. He was sure she would be furious. He had to think about himself. Rita Odena Lay wasn't planning to marry Maggie Fuller. She had her sights set on him. He was dodging and weaving trying his best to stay out of them.

Luther hit the bottom step of the porch at a dead run. His horse was tied up at the front hitching rail, but it seemed despondent, and in truth it was. Since Belle had left, the horse was deeply depressed, so he was unresponsive to Luther. Luther hurried to untie the stallion's reins. Then he heard the clomp of boot hit the wooden front porch. He looked over his shoulder. Rita was right behind him.

"Arrgh!" yelled Luther, and he sprinted for the barn.

Rita marched right behind him, the hem of her wedding dress dragging in the dirt. She did not notice. Luther was going to marry her, whether he wanted to or not. She could tell he was horrified at the idea, but Rita had taken such a reaction into account. Not that it didn't hurt. It did. She had gone to too much trouble to lose Luther Van Buren III, now. She would be Rita Van

Buren before nightfall. She grabbed a length of rope from her saddle, as she passed by her horse. She just wished her brothers were here to see the wedding. For a brief moment, Rita worried about her little brothers, but the thought did not last. The Lay family was never very sentimental.

Right before Luther got to the barn, Rita wound the rope into a lasso. The rope flew with marvelous precision through the air and landed with a plop around Luther's midsection. As Rita walked forward, she tightened the rope. Luther could struggle all he wanted. It only made the rope tighter.

"Get over here, Luther," Rita said.

"Never. You lied to me. I will never marry you," Luther said.

"You will marry me one way or the other."

"You will have to shoot me first, and then you will not be able to marry me."

"Luther, in these parts, no one will tell the difference. You could be dead for six months, and nobody would say a word. If'n they do, I'll just tell them I kilt you defending my honor. The Code of the West will protect me."

Luther did not know any more about the Code of the West than he had read about in dime novels, so what Rita said made some sense. He did not care, though. The thought of being married to this loud-mouth harridan was more than he could bear.

"Climb up on your horse," Rita said, poking him with his pistol. She led him over to the stallion. The horse stood fifteen hands, at least. There was no way he could mount the horse without using his hands.

Rita pulled Luther close to one side of the horse. Taking the rope, she circled to the other side. She pulled the rope with all her might, yanking Luther over the side of the horse. He was almost on. Then, she lumbered around to Luther's backside and using both hands, she shoved his rear up and onto the saddle.

"Madam!" he cried. "I am mortified."

"No, you ain't. You are Luther." Rita rushed around the horse to peer up into Luther's eyes. "You didn't hit your head, or anything did you, my darling?"

Luther groaned, and the sound pissed Rita clean off.

"We are headed for the priest. We's going to get married."

Luther felt a glimmer of hope. No priest in his right mind would marry them. He almost smiled, thinking how he would talk himself out of this situation.

"Come on. Let's ride. We's wasting daylight. The good padre closes the church in just a couple of hours." Rita took off on her horse, with Luther riding trussed up behind her. Soon they were at a one-story, flea-infested wooden building. Sure enough, a hand-painted sign nailed to the middle porch post declared the building a church. The Church of the EMakUlut Mary.

No one in their real mind would have ever believed that this was a read church, but it served the outlaw priest well. Most of his congregation could not read anyway. The rest, like the good padre, needed a safe place to hole up for a while, until whatever law or vigilante had left Brown's Hole. The evening bell had just begun to ring, and a young boy rushed to take Rita's horse.

Luther struggled to raise his head to see the priest. Soon a tall, black-garbed man waddled out to greet them. He was more over-weight than any clergy Luther had ever seen. The prêtre was wheezing with each step. Luther was afraid the man's heart would stop before he had a chance to speak his part. The good father knelt, so he could get a better look at Luther's face.

Luther was just as able to get a good gander at the priest. What he saw was not reassuring. The priest was the male, spitting image of Rita Odena Lay—except he was not quite as ugly.

"Is this the groom, Rita?" the padre asked.

"Yes, brother dear, this is him...and he's dying to marry me."

Her brother laughed. "I think I can see that. Let me ask you, is he dying to marry you, or is he going to die *or* marry you?'

"Don't be mudding the water with a bunch of talk. Marry us now," she said.

"Get him off the horse and bring him into the church." The priest sighed and waddled back the way he had come.

Rita pulled the rope holding Luther to the horse. He fell off the back of the stallion face first. She held out her hand and pulled him to his feet.

"Let's go, Luther."

Rita led him to the front altar. Luther looked at her but wisely kept his mouth shut for once.

"Get after it, brother," said Rita.

The priest intoned the ceremony, until he came to the part where he asked Luther, "Luther, do you take Rita to be your wife?"

Luther said, "No."

Just like that. The word was out.

A loud click resounded throughout the nave, as Rita thumbed the hammer back on Luther's pistol. She leaned next to his ear and whispered, "Would you like to change your mind?"

Chapter Twenty-eight

Even though Pearl had taken out after Range Detective Bill Puckett, trying to follow him to her pa's cattle, she soon realized that she had no idea which way he went. She had ridden past him out of Lockjaw's Trading Post. At the time, she had been buck-naked and not in the mood for hunting down Puckett. Now, dressed and ready, she could not figure out where in tarnation and hellfire he was.

Pearl rode Belle back in the direction she had seen Puckett riding. There was really no way to follow him from the trading post. There were too many tracks going in every different direction imaginable, so Pearl decided to go back to Miss Maggie's and see if she could backtrack Rita's trail. Pearl figured that Rita had come from the cattle into town. Maybe she could get a scent of which way that female polecat had traveled.

It only took Pearl a few minutes to reach the Fuller House; but as soon as she did, she knew something was wrong. Bill Puckett's mustang was tied to the hitching post. She could hear screams coming from the house. She leaned over Belle, quieting her; and almost on tiptoe, the two of them went through the open door of the barn.

Pearl's heart was pounding so hard, she felt like it would burst from her chest as she slid down from her saddle. She grabbed her Winchester and reloaded. Bolstered by the false courage she had drunk at Lockjaw's, she threw back her head and recklessly headed for the house. That Puckett was going to eat a plate load of lead, if he hurt one hair on Miss Maggie's head. By the way Miss Maggie was yelling, he was doing more than a little hair pulling.

Miss Maggie was hollering something horrible, and Pearl noticed that one of the hounds was lying in a pool of blood on the porch. She could not see the other dog at first. He was cowering under the far end of the wooden porch, as close as he could get to the house. Pearl hoped like hell he wouldn't start braying and miraculously he didn't. Instead, as she circled around the house deciding where was the best way to go in, the hound started to follow her.

"Hey, old boy. Can you help me?" Pearl whispered. "I need to kill that varmint what's in there and rescue your ma." Pearl eased around to the back of the house and angled up onto the porch. For all she knew, Puckett might not be alone, so she moved against the wall, scanning the yard for any other horses or hardcases. Nothing.

No matter how quietly she tried to walk, her boots faintly echoed on the wood floor, so she shucked them off and went on barefoot through the kitchen door. Even in the kitchen, the floor was mighty cold. Pearl silently hopped around, trying to stand the bitter cold flooring. Inside the house, she could hear Puckett hitting Miss Maggie. Something in Pearl's heart formed a hard know of hate.

She would kill that heathen polecat, if it was the last thing she ever did. Miss Maggie screamed once more, and it was the most horrible sound Pearl had ever heard. She took off running into the front of the house, hollering like a wild Indian and working the lever of the Winchester. The blood hound was right behind her.

Bill Puckett was standing over Miss Maggie holding a knife to her face. On her right cheek was a line of blood where the bastard had cut her. He reeled around and reared back to throw the knife at Pearl.

"Maggie, move!" Pearl yelled.

As Maggie slid to the floor and out of the way, Pearl threw the Winchester up and fired. She blew the knife clean out of Puckett's hand, taking a couple of fingers with it. The range detective squealed like a baby pig. Then the hound was on him. Pearl ran to Miss Maggie's side scooping up the little woman and hurrying toward the kitchen. She sat Maggie at the kitchen table and handed her a towel.

"Where's your gun, Miss Maggie?" Pearl asked.

Maggie pointed at a shelf near the stove. "He snuck up on me, or I'd have shot him myself."

Pearl could tell that Miss Maggie was more angry than scared. Pearl handed her the gun. "Keep that ready, in case the bastard gets me. I'm headed back to finish what I started."

The hound was braying loud and long, but then Pearl head a sound that caused her blood to freeze. A whimper. The knife. She knew without being told that Bill Puckett had stabbed the hound. Afraid of what she would find but determined to forge ahead, Pearl strode the length of the hall headed for the living room. She worked the lever of her Winchester again. This time she would finish this owl hoot off. She would shoot him dead and then sing at his funeral.

Pearl hesitated for just a moment at the parlor door. She could hear the hound moaning, so she knew he was still alive. She pulled the rifle close to her chest. When she opened the door, she intended to go in firing for all she was worth. Hatred worked its way up from its pit in her guts. Pearl kicked the door and jumped into the open doorway.

Puckett's ass was headed out a window. The chicken-livered coward had slid open a front window and was escaping to the front porch. The hound's throat was cut. His blood was slowly seeping into the new rag rug on the floor. Fire flashed from Pearl's Winchester.

Puckett screamed and fell the rest of the way out of the window. He grabbed his buttocks and ran like a scalded dog to his mustang. With his mangled hand, he tried to hold his reins but couldn't. The other hand was hanging on to the hole in his britches, as the mustang slung him this way and that. Pearl worked the Winchester again. The click of her lever was the only sound Puckett heard. He grabbed the reins with his good hand and rode like the devil was after him.

Pearl lowered her rifle and fell to the floor beside the old hound dog. His eyes looked deeply into hers, almost begging her to save his life. Her fingers slid to the wound encircling his throat, feeling their way around the cut. It wasn't that deep. If she could get the big hound into the kitchen maybe she could help him.

Adrenalin raced through Pearl's veins. She could do it. Squaring her shoulders, Pearl picked up the large dog and waddled into the kitchen. As though she was holding a baby instead of a full-grown hound, Pearl laid the beast on the kitchen table.

"Miss Maggie, I think we can save him," said Pearl.

Maggie ran to her beloved blood hound. She threw her arms around his neck. "Beauregard, you old coot. That mean ole polecat almost got you."

"That bastard Puckett killed the other dog, but I'm sure this one will live."

Miss Maggie looked into Beauregard's eyes. They were soulful but alert. "I think you're right, Pearl." She went to business right then, cleaning the dog's wound and grabbing her needle to stitch him up. "Get out of here, Pearl. Go and get those cattle, before Bill Puckett or Rita Lay get there first."

"Miss Maggie..."

"I said git. I've got my gun handy, now. If'n that bastard comes back, I'll put a hole where his heart is supposed to be. Go!"

"What about the law, Miss Maggie? Don't you want me to fetch the law?" Pearl asked.

Miss Maggie laughed. "The only law in these parts is that of the fastest gun. Shoot first, Pearl, and ask questions later. That son of a biscuit eater needs to know who's boss. So does that soiled dove, Rita. Shoot 'em, Pearl. Shoot 'em both dead."

Chapter Twenty-nine

Madder than a couple of hornets, Pearl and Belle hit the road again hunting for Bill Puckett. That buzzard-head had gotten away from her this time, but Pearl would be damned if he would do it twice. She dug her heels into Belle's side, pressing the mare into a rip-stomping gallop. The little mare obliged. Soon they were gaining on Puckett.

For a moment, a little rise hid him from view. As Pearl topped it, the wily coyote and his mustang sprang toward her from the side. The bastard was trying to ram her. Belle was a sharp little horse, and she skittered to one side, throwing their attackers off. Pearl grabbed for her Winchester. She took hold of the barrel and swung her rifle like a club, using both hands. At the last minute, Puckett's horse swerved to the side.

Pearl clinched her saddle with her knees. Belle turned around and headed full charge toward Puckett and the mustang. Like gladiators of old, this was a fight to the death. Pearl and Belle were locked in the most dangerous conflict of their young lives. This time when Pearl came alongside Puckett, the stock of the rifle hit him square in the head, almost knocking him off the horse.

Before she could even think, Pearl felt Belle barrel into the side of the mustang. Using the momentum from the attack, Pearl leapt from her horse, landing on Puckett's back. Somehow, she had lost the Winchester in the scuffle, but it did not matter. She reached her hands around Bill Puckett's head and clawed at his face, trying to get to his eyes. Like a mighty savage, Pearl intended to gouge out his eyes and rip off his scalp

Puckett was a gunslinger and worse. Pearl had no intention of letting him turn his six guns on her. A blind gunslinger was a dead gunslinger. Her fingers explored his cheek bones, ripping his skin and probing for his eyes. The range detective swung his body back and forth trying with all his might to dislodge the hellcat on his back. Finally, Pearl managed to jab him hard in the left eye.

Puckett hollered out her name and grabbed at Pearl's hands. She wouldn't let go. He threw his arms backward. The action tossed Pearl from his back and off his horse. Puckett did not wait around to finish the fight, and that was all that saved him.

Pearl hit the dirt road hard. She jumped to her feet, staggered a couple of steps, and grabbed for her knife. Puckett was long gone. His horse, Pistol, was moving down the road, and Puckett wasn't looking back. Pearl spied her Winchester a few yards away. As she walked over to fetch it, she watched that polecat Puckett ride for his life.

Belle sprang to Pearl's side, ready to ride after the lowlife and charge him again, but Pearl was tired. Bone tired. Too much had happened. She knew she needed every drop of energy she possessed to save her pa's cattle. They were hidden somewhere in this god-forsaken place. It was her job to find them. As much as she wanted to get rid of Puckett and even to see Rita hanging from a tree, she wanted to find those cattle.

Pearl figured her pa would never really respect her, until she could prove her mettle. She knew she had what it took to be a rancher, but he did not. He saw her as fit for cooking and washing and working her fingers to the bone for him, but he didn't see her as an equal. Pearl wanted him to recognize that she was as capable a rancher as any man.

She shook off her feelings and concentrated on the task at hand—find those cattle. More than once, she had heard about how good the grazing was in the western corner of Brown's Hole. With a quick glance at the sun, she headed north and then angled back to the west. Before she knew it, Pearl had ridden to the edge of a great basin. Spread out below were the cattle. A quick head count revealed that none save one had been lost. Then Pearl saw the young bull.

An outlaw rustler and two of his compadres had just roped him and laid him on the ground. Pearl's gut clenched tight, as one of the outlaws tied the bull's legs together and another lifted a running brand from the fire. The brand was red hot, and the young bull bawled loudly when the hot metal met the edge of his rear end. The Pecker Brand had just been changed forever.

Pearl felt like that running brand had seared her heart. She raised her rifle and sighted in on the rustler. He was tall and wore a green-checkered shirt. Idly, she noticed that the elbows of the shirt were patched. She wondered if he had a wife somewhere waiting at home, patching another shirt. She was too mad to care. She worked the lever of the Winchester. Smoke bellowed from its barrel, and the outlaw rustler hit the ground. Dead. His running brand spinning in the dirt.

The other two hardcases saw Pearl and started firing. For a moment, she stayed put—a lone silhouette of horse and rider outlined against the darkening sky. Then as if in defense of Pearl, the great sky opened up in peals of thunder, and lightning shot through the sky behind her. To the desperados below, she looked powerful. Buoyed by adrenalin and another shot of Miss Petunia's Potion and Elixir, she felt that way, too.

Pearl pulled back hard on Belle's reins, and then she charged, riding at the outlaws for all she was worth. The Winchester flashed again. One and then the other rustler was dead.

When these outlaws had aligned themselves with Rustlin' Rita, they had chosen the wrong woman. Pearl was not afraid of them. She damn sure wasn't going to let them get away with her pa's cattle. Rita she would deal with later. These bad hombres had it coming, now.

The young bull was bawling like a baby and thrashing to be let loose of his ropes. Pearl rode into the makeshift branding camp and slid from her horse beside the bull. Frantically, he strained trying to get free. Pearl dropped to her knees beside him and laid her strong hand against his shoulder. Immediately, the bull began to calm down. His big brown eyes met hers, and she could tell he knew who she was.

The bodies of the three outlaws were scattered around the fire. Pearl looked at one ugly mug after another; she could not recognize any of their faces. No money to be made from this bunch. They were probably just drifters that Rita had hired to help her brand the cattle.

Well, the Pecker cattle were not going to be sold with a slow brand. Pa would have his cattle back, and she would have his respect. Pearl stood and rolled the body of the man who had handled the brand away from the fire, so she could untie the young bull. She pulled the rope free. The bull sprang to his feet, almost knocking her down.

Faster than a jack rabbit, another bad hombre rode into the camp. He launched himself on top of Pearl. His action had thrown Pearl back, close enough to the fire to smell her hair singeing. Pearl could not catch her breath. The heavy body of the man on top of her kept her from moving.

"You filthy bastard," she gasped.

"Watch your mouth, woman," he said and slapped her hard.

Tears flashed into Pearl's eyes, and she didn't know what made her madder. That this worthless sack of cow crap had hit her or that she had cried. A moment later, it ceased to matter. The greasy varmint was grinning and pulling at her vest.

"Let's see what you've got under here," he said. As the vest opened, the little Derringer popped into view and then slid out of the vest down to Pearl's hand. She scrambled to grab it. The outlaw grabbed for it at the same time, but he was too late. Pearl raised the revolver and shot him right in the face. Screaming and clutching his eye, the mangy varmint fell to one side. Pearl pushed him as hard as she could, rolling him off her. Then she jumped to her feet and shot him again.

"I cain't believe it," Pearl said. "Has every man in Brown's Hole lost his cotton pickin' mind, today?" She took a second look at the critter who had attacked her. He was one of Chet Miller's cousins. Her mind flashed back to the scene in front of Lockjaw Lemmings' trading post. Chet's *three* cousins had ridden up. There were more of these rascals around.

"I got to get a move on," Pearl said. "Belle, come here. Let's get these cattle herded up and the hell out of here before the rest of Chet Miller's rustling relatives show up."

Belle stood ready as Pearl swung up and into the saddle. The cattle were grazing over the west end of the basin, so it was not too difficult to start rounding them up closer together. Pearl had no idea how she would drive the cattle back down to Vernal. She needed some help—at least two or three good men. She wasn't sure she could find them in Brown's Hole. She reckoned Lockjaw Lemmings could help her out there. She moved the cattle toward the edge of the pasture.

During the melee, Pearl had not noticed that the sky had grown darker. Thick clouds gathered overhead, and the first sprinkling of cold, slushy rain began to fall. Pearl headed the cattle closer to the edge of the basin. Frantically looking for shelter from the approaching storm, she missed the more serious threat awaiting her atop the rim of the basin.

Chet Miller's cousins had found an ally even more evil than their mother-killing cousin. This hombre hated Pearl's very guts and livers. Puckett. Range Detective Bill Puckett had managed to join up with two of the vilest cattle rustling critters in Brown's Hole. To a man, they had every reason to want to kill Pearl Hawthorne. Together, they rode down the steep embankment headed straight for Pearl.

Belle spotted the trio before Pearl did. She skittered to the left and let out a sharp whinny, trying to warn her mistress. It was too late. Just as the sky let loose its load, Puckett rode into the lead. The other two villainous desperados fanned out, stopping the cattle from moving forward.

"Yee-hah!" Pearl shouted. "Come on, boys, keep a moving." She still had not seen Puckett or the cousins.

The cattle did not budge. She rode through the herd, trying to figure out what the trouble with Belle was. Then she saw them. As Puckett leveled his rifle to shoot her, Pearl leaned low in the saddle and kicked the cow nearest to her. It commenced bawling and slammed into a nearby bull. Suddenly, all hell broke loose. Cattle charged at one another, and even Mother Nature decided to take Pearl's side.

Lightning streaked through the sky. Pearl had never heard such thundering in all her life. She swung Belle around, moving through the surge of animals to the open flatland. She glanced behind her. Puckett was too busy trying to stop the angry barrage of cattle to come after her now.

Pearl needed help. She kicked Belle into a gallop. She rode back toward the trail to the trading post. Maybe Lockjaw would know where she could find some able-bodied men to help get her cattle back and drive them home to Vernal. In the meantime, she needed a place to hole up and regroup.

Briefly, Pearl wondered what had happened to Third Luther. Would he really get hitched to that soiled dove, Rustlin' Rita? She shook her head and rode harder. Why did she care?

Chapter Thirty

Luther was looking down the wrong end of his very own Colt revolver. Ironically, his gun was a Peacemaker, but Rustlin' Rita Odena Lay had anything but peacemaking on her mind.

"Did you hear me, Luther darling? I asked if'n you'd like to change your mind."

The preacher coughed and thumped his Bible. "I ain't got all day, Rita," he said. "Is you getting married or not?"

"Shut up, you idiot. Of course, we's getting married." She waved the gun at Luther. "Ain't that right, honey?"

Luther panicked. He looked at the face of the preacher and into the piggish little eyes of fiancée, and he puked. Upchucked all over Rita's fancy white-lace wedding gown. With a shrill scream that made both Luther and the preacher grab for their ears, Rita threw the gun at Luther and clutched her skirt. Vomit was running down the courses of lace on the wedding dress faster than Luther lit a shuck out of that church. In one smooth move he wiped his face, bowed in apology, grabbed his gun and hit the door.

"My dress! My beautiful wedding dress!" Rita wailed and spun around and around in horrified dismay. Then she stopped and looked at the swinging door of the chapel. Luther was long gone, and she knew he had no plans of ever marrying her.

"What the hell did he eat?" the outlaw priest asked. "That's the most god-awful thing I've ever smelled—smells like burnt rabbit and something else. Lord a mercy."

"Ruination. That's what this is. Just pure-dee ruination." Rita grabbed the waistline of the wedding dress with both hands and ripped it down. She stepped out of the skirt, wearing nothing but the bodice and a pair of red flannel bloomers. "I'm going to kill that Boston bastard, if it's the last thing I ever do."

Tears were running down Rita's face, making her cheeks puffy and swollen. Her nose started running, so she turned to the side and held first one nostril and then the other, as she blew the excess snot from her nose. For a brief moment, she was glad that Luther couldn't see her, but it didn't much matter now. He had run like a plucked chicken awaiting a wringing, and he wouldn't ever come back to her.

Then Rita had a terrible thought. "He's running back to Pearl. That sorry pathetic little tooth-pulling doctor is going after her." She turned to her brother. "Saddle up. We's going to have some fun. We are going to find that puke bag dentist *and* that milkmaid Pearl Hawthorn. We'll kill them both. If'n I cain't have him, she cain't have him, neither."

"You ain't wearing that get up; I hope," said her brother. "You smell something terrible. I've got some trousers in the back you can have."

"We ain't got time for dilly-dallying," Rita said and went on out the door. "Let's go. It's starting to rain, and he's getting away."

The preacher stepped over the ruined remnant of Rita's wedding dress and followed her to the door. One glance at the sky and his mind was made up. "I ain't going with you," he said.

"What the hell? Why not?"

"I just ain't. That's all. It ain't my fight, and I don't want to come." He pointed at the sky. "Look at that. It's going to come a blowout rain in about thirty minutes. Then the whole countryside is going to freeze over. I'm staying put." He turned around and went back into the chapel.

"If'n you wasn't my brother and a preacher, I'd shoot you dead, you bastard." Rita didn't notice the rain or the cold just then. She was fired up and red hot to catch Luther and to kill Pearl. If there was one thing she hated, it was a runaway fiancé. It was not like this was the first time it had happened to her; but if she had anything to do about it, it would be the last damn time.

Meanwhile, Luther had never felt such revulsion. Vomiting in public was not a correct Englishman's style. Still, it had provided him the opening he needed to escape. On reflection, he realized that during a shotgun wedding proper decorum was not conducive to a fast getaway. If Luther had to choose, he would take vomiting over marrying Rita any day. He shuddered to think how close he had come to being wed to such a hooligan. He would much rather be married to Pearl than to Rita.

He yanked the reins of the stallion almost throwing himself overboard. Married to Pearl? Preposterous. Where had the thought come from? Pearl wasn't set on marrying him. So, what put such a thought into his head? Sure, she had saved his life on more than one occasion. That was just her nature. Luther smiled remembering how Pearl had curled up against him in the cavern to keep him warm.

Then he thought of Rita. He heeled the stallion into a trot and headed for the trading post. There was no point in getting caught a second time. Rita might be right behind him. He needed a place to hide out, until he could find Pearl.

Leaving the makeshift church and his soiled bride behind, Luther rode for Lockjaw's and sanctuary. As he pulled up to the hitching post of the trading post, he looked at Chet Miller's buckskin still tied up in front. He wondered who would claim the animal. It was a good-looking horse and would probably fetch a good price. By right, he thought is should be Pearl's.

"Mr. Lemmings," Luther called out. "I say, Mr. Lemmings, are you about, sir?"

Lockjaw burst through the door. He had attempted to clean the soot off his face. His hair looked even darker and greasier, as did his clothes. "What the hell do you want? It ain't been a good day, mister."

"I'll say the same," said Luther. "I need a place to hide out for a while. My former fiancée, Rita Odena Lay, is after me." He coughed and looked away. "I seem to have left her at the church."

Lockjaw threw back his head and hee-hawed like a jackass. "You poor dumb son of a bitch. Are you telling me you left Rustlin' Rita at the altar? You as good as dead. Damn, and I done run out of coffins." Lockjaw scratched at his mangy beard and thought.

"Mr. Lockjaw, I need a place to secure my animal." Luther pointed at his horse. "It seems all too visible at the moment."

"No shit. She sees that horse, and she'll ride in here shooting anything that moves." The ramifications of what he had just said struck Lockjaw like an iron skillet to his addled brain. "Well, get that critter round back and out of sight. Are you stupid, man?"

Luther grabbed the reins and turned to lead his horse around to the rear of the trading post. "Are you certain we'll be safe here?"

"Hell, you ain't safe nowhere, but standing here jawing about it could get us both killed." He pointed to the side of the building. "Get a move on. Put that pony in the stable out back and get your ass hid under something."

The horse was quickly stashed in the barn. Luther was looking around for a spot of cover, when he heard someone ride up. He could not make out what the person was saying, but he was sure of one thing. It was a female, and she was headed straight for the barn.

Quickly, he jumped behind a feed stall and got down on hands and knees, crawling toward the ladder to the haymow. Bits of straw and dust formed little clouds around him as he scuttled to the back.

The door of the barn opened, creating a crack of light and letting in the cold outside air. Luther paused for just a moment. Then as quietly as he could, he scooted along the floor. He heard the familiar click of the Winchester's lever before he heard her voice.

"Don't make another move, you varmint, or I'll split your britches with one shot."

Chapter Thirty-one

Luther froze. He was in a most embarrassing position. He started to turn around, but then a bullet split a chunk of wood off the support post to his right. The Winchester's lever cranked again.

"Third Luther, I'm a warning you. I'm having to decide whether to let you live or send you out like the chicken-livered corpse you deserve to be," Pearl said.

"What did I do?" Luther asked.

"Hmm. Let me think for just a gall-dern second. Seems I remember you crawling the last time I seen you—crawling up under a bed while your crazy cattle rustling fiancée tried to blow holes in me."

"I was merely trying to find safety."

Pearl harrumphed. "Sure, you were. Either you're a despicable coward, or you were in cahoots with that wench and was helping her kill me. Which was it, Third Luther?"

Luther looked down at the dirt floor of the barn and considered his options. "When you put it like that, I am immensely ashamed and deserve your scorn and your hatred. I am a coward and worse. Less than a man."

He sat down on the ground and looked up at Pearl. His handsome face was flushed with shame. The barrel of the Winchester came down. Nothing was said as Pearl looked at Luther's face. No matter how angry and disappointed in him she was, she just could not shoot him. She knew that later she might regret not blowing his fool head off. At that moment all she could think of was a rabbit burnt to smithereens inside a soot covered pan.

"Get up, you polecat. I cain't shoot you when you look all hang dog like that. Damnation and tarnation, Third Luther, you do try a woman. You really do." The Winchester dropped to her side.

Luther stood and walked up so close to Pearl she could count every eyelash—every long, dark eyelash. He blinked, and her stomach did a crazy somersault. Not for the first time, Pearl had to remind herself what an idiot Third Luther could be. Still, there was something about him, when he had that hurt little boy look.

Without thinking, she raised the rifle up level with Luther's stomach. "Get that there look off your face, Third Luther."

He ignored her. "Madam, would you please accept my deepest apologies." He stepped even closer.

"If'n you come one step closer, you won't need a belt no more."

His face was so near to hers that he was almost kissing her. She could feel his breath as he said, "I'm sorry, Pearl. In the future, if I have a future, I will never desert you again. I mean it."

Time seemed frozen. They were so close—so very, very close.

The great wooden door of the barn creaked once before it slammed against the wall, knocking hoes and shovels and pitchforks to the floor. Framed in the opening was a hell of a figure. Wearing the top half of an elaborate wedding gown coupled with bright red flannel bloomers, the demon in the doorway screamed once. Then, it grabbed for a pitchfork and waited, poised and evil, to take the soul of her runaway darling.

Without a doubt, Rita was the most terrifying sight that either Luther or Pearl had ever seen. She looked like an escapee from the gates of hell. Her hair was stiff and matted, and it seemed to stand on end. Pearl and Luther broke apart, their almost kiss forgotten. They ran like rats running from a hungry cat. Pearl headed for the haymow. She shimmied up the wooden ladder leading to it in a second.

Luther, though, was caught against the side door. Rita had not taken any chances; she had bolted the door from the outside. She shoved the pitchfork forward and walked toward him. Each step was slow...deliberate. Murder was in her eyes, and if Luther didn't come up with a plan, he was a goner for sure.

Pearl's words echoed in Luther's mind. She thought he was a coward and a cheat. He found the notion that she thought he was a failure unbearable, so he did something entirely out of character. Like a real gunfighter, he drew the Colts from his holster and took his stand.

"You ain't going to shoot me, darling," Rita drawled. "You ain't got it in you."

"Stay where you are," Luther said.

Pearl moved to the edge of the loft to watch. She had no plans to help Luther. He was on his own. For Pearl, it was now or never. Luther would either be a man or turn yellow belly and run. She waited to see what would happen.

Luther thumbed the hammers back on the pair of Peacemakers. "I said to stay put, Rita."

Rita slowly angled closer. There was hate in her heart and puke on her dress. "I loved you, Luther. You betrayed me. Ain't no man going to do that to Rita Odena Lay and live."

Errant thoughts flitted through Luther's mind. Unfortunately for him, they showed on his face. He found Rita disgusting. He was also afraid. He grabbed the butts of the pistols tighter. His teeth gritted together. He took a step forward.

"Shove off, Rita, and you won't get hurt."

"Hurt!" she cried. "You're the one about to be hurt." With that she thrust the pitchfork in front of her and ran straight for him.

The roar of the Colts startled everything living in the barn. Luther's horse broke free of its stall and ran for the door. Pearl turned from the edge of the loft and vaulted into a pile of fresh hay. And Rita...Rita threw the pitchfork into the air and ran for cover behind a feed stall.

Luther was likely the most surprised of all. Never in his life had he deliberately shot at anyone. Until today. He had missed his target totally, but he had stood up to Rita. He strutted up to Rita and pointed the gun at her again.

"Get out, Rita. I don't want to have to hurt you. I will never marry you," Luther said. "Just go away and never come back."

Pearl crawled from the hay. Let Rita go? Had that idiot really lost his cotton-picking mind? She leapt from the loft, landing right between Rita and Luther.

"She ain't going nowhere. Except to hell," Pearl said. She flipped the Winchester and pointed it at Rita. "I could give you a gut shot right now that would take days for you to die from. How about that, Rustlin' Rita? How's about I shoot you in your fat belly?

Out of the blue, Luther moved behind Pearl and grabbed her shoulders. "Pearl, you can't shoot her. That would be wrong."

As Pearl looked over her shoulder to contradict Luther, Rita knocked the barrel of the Winchester aside and threw herself on top of Pearl. Rita grabbed Pearl's hair with both hands and pulled like she intended to yank Pearl bald.

"Sheee-it!" screamed Pearl. She slammed her fist into Rita's nose.

Blood and snot went everywhere, but Pearl did not care. She rammed Rita's nose again, and then she grabbed Rita's hair, pulling it for all she was worth. Round and round, the two women screeched and yanked each other's hair. Finally, Pearl was able to maneuver Rita against the wall. She commenced to slam Rita's head repeatedly into the wooden barrier.

Unbeknownst to Pearl, Rita's head was harder than a brick. Rita feigned a faint, and Pearl let go of her hair. Roaring, Rita head-butted Pearl, knocking her to the ground. Rita headed for the pitchfork, aiming to poke more than one hole in Pearl. Just as she managed to grab the long wooden handle, Pearl jumped to her feet and ran up next to Rita. With a swift sidekick, Pearl was able to sweep Rita's feet out from under her.

"Ladies, please," said Luther.

"Shut up," said Pearl and Rita together.

Rita landed hard against a metal bucket full of horse feed. Her face bounced against the side of the bucket. Blood spurted down the front of her dress top. As Rita struggled to stand, it was obvious that her left front tooth was dangling in its socket. Pearl leaned against the side of the feed stall and patted Luther's horse. She looked at Rita and then at Luther.

"Rita Odena Lay, you are under arrest," Pearl said. She fished her badge from her coat pocket and held it up for Rita to see. "But first, you might want to see a dentist."

Chapter Thirty-two

While Luther worked on Rita's tooth, Pearl gathered supplies from the trading post. It seemed like every step she took Lockjaw took with her. Pearl could not seem to shake him no matter what she said or did. Seeing Pearl naked had changed Lockjaw Lemmings—at least for the time being. He was more polite and certainly more generous.

"Lockjaw, I got my bounty money to buy supplies. Nothing more. Don't be trying to load me up with anything I don't really need," Pearl said.

"Never, Pearl. I wouldn't..." he stammered, "uh, ever. How about some pemmican? I got some made up of venison. It's mighty good." He could not take his eyes off her.

"Would you quit staring at me? I feel like the only hen in a yard full of roosters," she shouted at him. "And thankee, I'll take the pemmican and some salt pork, too. If'n you got it."

"Yes, I have it. You ought to have plenty of grub, if'n you're going back home to Vernal. Too bad about your cattle, though."

Pearl spun around. "What about my cattle? I know where they are. They're up on the west end of the basin, but Puckett and them cousins of Chet's has got them. I don't know how they hell they's planning to keep 'em moving in this rain. I reckoned that I could hire me some hombres and take 'em back before everything thaws out."

"Hmm, once the sun comes out, it ain't going to be nothing but mud up there," Lockjaw said. "But you got bigger problems than that. I heard tell that Puckett has put a price on your head and that city boy back there." He motioned toward Luther.

"What? What's the charge? He cain't just put a bounty on somebody's head for no good reason," Pearl said. She thought about it for a moment, and then laughed it off. "I ain't done nothing, and Luther for damn sure ain't."

She piled her supplies on the trading post counter—bacon, sugar, coffee, soda crackers, a bottle of whiskey, and two of elixir. She also purchased a small amount of lard, oatmeal, boiled eggs, and some beans. The trip to Vernal should only take several days on the trail; but with the cattle, Pearl was adding on at least an extra day. Game was plentiful, and she knew fresh meat would not be much of a problem to find.

Lockjaw wasn't named Lockjaw for nothing. He shut his mouth up tighter than Job's hatband and went about adding up the charges for the supplies. But his face spoke volumes. As Pearl looked at the set of his face, she started to wonder what old greasy head knew that she didn't.

"How's he got a bounty on me?" she asked.

Lockjaw grabbed for some candy canes in a bowl under the counter. "Sweets for the sweetheart?"

"Hell, Lockjaw, tell me what that son of a biscuit eater is up to now." Pearl grabbed Lockjaw by the collar of his shirt but just as quickly let go. The storekeeper was still covered in soot.

"It's just that he writ up a sign is all." Lockjaw Lemmings mumbled and pointed to the front door.

Pearl stomped to the batwings and slammed her way through them. "Mother of Sweet Jesus," she hissed. "That low down pond sucking varmint has done it now! I'm going to shoot that polecat and mount his head above my very bed. That's what I'm going to do."

Lockjaw turned to Luther who was trying to hang on to Rita and fix her tooth at the same time. "You best get done with that dental fixing and get on the road, fore every two-bit bounty hunter in these here parts is after you."

The batwings bounced open. Pearl marched back to the counter holding the poster. She threw her money on the counter and held up the posters. "Have you read this?" she screamed at Lockjaw.

"Well, Pearl, I don't exactly read all that good."

"Let me read it to you. Wanted: The Vigilante Vixen and the Boston Bad Man. Pearl Hawthorne and Luther Van Buren III. Wanted for Murder, Attempted Murder of a Range Detective, Cattle Rustling, and Obscene Nakedness. Reward of $200. $100 each for the arrest and conviction of the outlaws."

"Obscene what? Who was naked?" Luther asked and almost shoved his finger down Rita's throat. As Rita gagged and choked on his finger, Luther grabbed hold of her hair trying to hold her steady. The end result was a slapping contest. Rita hauled off and hit Luther; and before he thought to act like a gentleman, he slapped her back.

For a moment, Pearl was dumbstruck. Fear formed low in her belly. Then a burning fire began to rage in her chest. Her ears felt like they were going to pop right out of her head. That dad-burned detective was going to get his comeuppance. Oh yes, he was. If Pearl could have laid eyes on him right then, she would have shot him where he'd never tell. Her fingers itched with the desire to blow him away.

"Who has seen this sign?" She waved the poster at Lockjaw.

"Ummm," he considered. "Not too many folks. Maybe eight or twelve of the regulars. Look at the bright side. At least there ain't a picture."

She looked at him, until he started to fidget.

"Oh, and them relatives of Chet Miller's, but you already know they's hooked up with Puckett. Oh, and them sons of Earp somebody or other. I ain't rightly sure how many."

"You peckerwood," Pearl said. She breathed and leaned over the counter to get in Lockjaw's face. She pulled the Derringer from her vest, exposing a creamy glimpse of cleavage. She thumbed the hammer back on the little pistol and pointed it right at Lockjaw's nose. He did not even notice. His eyes were glued to the spot between her breasts.

"I ought to shoot you deader than Chet Miller on Sunday. You greasy polecat. You ain't even fit to kill," Pearl said. "And quit looking at my tits. You're making me feel funny."

"I could make you feel real good, Miss Pearl," Lockjaw said. He said it sort of dreamy-like, but when he took a gander at Pearl's face, he dove under the counter like an entire tribe of Indians was after his hair.

Rita picked that moment to try and escape. She pushed Luther away from her and ran for the back door. She picked the wrong place and the worse time. Pearl's gun was cocked and loaded. She fired the little gun at Rita's rear end. Whooping fit to bust, Rita grabbed her derriere and fled behind a pile of dry goods.

Crying and wailing, Rita crawled along the baseboards still trying to escape. Pearl reloaded the gun, as she walked around the corner of a large table.

"You better not make me chase you, Rita Odena Lay. Cos, I'm in a bad mood. Running after your sorry ass ain't going to make me feel any better."

Pearl motioned for Luther to go around the other way, so they could box Rita in between the dry goods and the pots and pans. Luther tip-toed past the coffee pots and was almost to the pots and pans, when Rita took off running. She cannoned into him, knocking him flat and racing for the back door. Blood was streaming from her tail end, but she didn't notice. Pearl fired another shot into the air, and Rita hit the ground.

"Don't kill me, Pearl," Rita begged.

Pearl went and stood over her. She kicked Rita in the rear making her yelp.

"What was that, Rita darling? I couldn't hear you," Pearl said sweetly.

"You heard me, Pearl. I said don't kill me."

"You better watch your tone, little missy. I don't like you. And have you clean forgot stealing my pa's cattle? Cos I ain't, and I feel like holding a grudge."

Lockjaw was standing by the swinging doors in front of the trading post, staring at four riders rapidly approaching the station. They were the Earp brothers, and they were coming in fast and furious.

"Pearl, you better quit your fighting and get on out of here. The Earp brothers has just pulled up to the hitching post," Lockjaw said. Hard footsteps clomped on the front porch. The vibrations of the men's footsteps could be felt in the trading post. He ran back inside the store to his counter. "Line up. Quick like I done arrested you myself. Hurry!"

Pearl grabbed Rita by the hair and pulled her to stand in between her and Luther. "Just keep your mouth shut, Rita, and maybe we can get out of this alive."

The trading post door swung open. Four of the ugliest hombres Pearl and Luther had ever seen walked inside. The ugliest one, the one with a nose that looked like it had been broken one too many times, spoke first.

"Who you got back there, Lockjaw?"

"I've got me some prisoners. Just caught 'em hiding out back in my barn."

"We heard about those two," another outlaw said, pointing at Pearl and Luther. "But who's the looker with them red knickers?"

The other outlaws snickered and pointed at Rita.

"Well, that there is Rustlin' Rita. I caught her, too. She's his fiancée," said Lockjaw, flipping his thumb in Luther's direction. "But never mind about them. Like I said, they's my prisoners. So, lessen you want some supplies or grub, you might as well head on out of here." Luther's voice had gone high and squeaky.

Pearl closed her eyes. She figured they were all as good as dead. Then Luther surprised them all.

As the vicious hombres drew closer, one of them pointed at Pearl and said, "That's the woman what gets nekkid. Let's take her clothes off and see for sure that it's really her."

Like a flash of lightning, Luther whipped his Colts from their holster and fired one into the ceiling of the trading post. The desperados ran for the door. Luther was firing first one gun and then the other. One of the outlaws turned to draw. By accident, Luther shot him square in the chest killing him instantly.

Pearl and Lockjaw grabbed for their rifles and started firing after the hard cases. No one noticed when Rita slipped out the back door. Holding her butt, she ran around the side of the trading post and grabbed the reins of her horse. It was not until the gun smoke cleared that Pearl realized that Rita was gone. By then, it really didn't matter.

Pearl and Luther were wanted. Pearl's cattle were still in the hands of Puckett and his hired guns. Pearl finished rustling up her supplies, paid off old greasy Lockjaw then headed out to reclaim her cattle.

The Vigilante Vixen and her Bad Man were hot on the trail of the cattle once again. This time, they were taking no prisoners. If Pearl found Bill Puckett and the cattle, she planned to shoot first and ask questions later.

Chapter Thirty-three

The sun was beginning to set when Pearl and Luther rode away from Lockjaw Lemmings' trading post. It looked like a blazing orange ball, as it sank low against the horizon. Waves of red, pink, and purple spread across the sky briefly illuminating the encroaching darkness. Pearl and Luther rode on. The night brought a teeth-shattering cold with it that crept into their bones and scorched the skin on their faces. It was a bitter, unrelenting cold that froze the rain-soaked ground, until it felt so hard that it would break.

"I wonder if those hard cases found some shelter for my cattle. Usually, the basin's warmer than the rest of Brown's Hole. With the rain, I'm worried that it is like a huge bowl holding the water in it," said Pearl.

"What happens then?" Luther asked.

"First, the ground turns to mud. Then it freezes around the cattle's feet. I don't want to find Pa's cattle just to see them die."

The pair rode on in silence for a while. All Pearl could think of was the cattle. She had taken care of them for the past few years, and she knew their faces and their personalities. Some folks might think her funny, but she really thought of the cattle as part of her family—a part her pa loved more than her. If she could rescue the cattle, he could not help but love her and respect her, too.

Now that Pearl had Chet Miller's horse along with her, things were more complicated. She needed a place to tie him up, a safe place, while she went after Bill Puckett and the rustlers.

"I think we should leave Miller's horse and the supplies with Miss Maggie, while we round up the cattle. It's pitch dark now, and we could eat something and head on after the herd," Pearl said.

"I had a similar thought, but you're in charge, Pearl. I just want you to know that I will help you in any way I can. I will delay my return home, until the cattle are safely back at your ranch."

Since Pearl had not had time to think about Luther returning to Boston, she was shocked to hear him talk about leaving. She frowned. Third Luther had come to feel like a partner to her, a partner that couldn't shoot straight to save his life and was sometimes as dumb as a post, but she had not thought about what life would be like without him. She was shocked at herself to find she did not like the idea of a life without Luther. Then the thought of her weakness had her mad as hell. What was he to her anyway but a nuisance and a distraction? She had a job to do, and she needed to get on with it.

"Thanks for that Third Luther. I reckon we can sit a spell at Miss Maggie's and come up with a plan. Bill Puckett and them men ain't going to hand over my cattle without a fight. We need us a plan, and we need to reload. I'll bet you shot up damn near every bullet you had in them guns."

"Yes, madam, you have a point. Still, we managed to scare off those bad guys," Luther said proudly.

Pearl glanced at him and laughed to herself. "You bet we did. You're becoming a gunslinger, Third Luther."

Luther blushed. "Well, I don't know about that..."

"I guess you are. You shot that man dead. Plus, we's both wanted now. We have to get Puckett, or he'll be after us forever."

Nothing else was said, as they galloped up to Miss Maggie's front porch. Pearl noticed that the body of the hound dog had been moved. Someone had tried to scrub off his blood. Four horses were tied to the hitching post, but they were not the roans ridden by the Earp brothers. She noticed the light coats of the horses. All except one. One of the animals was black with a gray mane. It was huge, and she instantly thought it looked like the horse of a devil. She pointed out the stallion to Luther. Pearl and Luther took their time dismounting. They kept looking at the black stallion.

"I wonder who owns that horse," Pearl whispered to Luther.

The front door of the Fuller House crashed open. In the doorway, stood a man as black and big as the horse. "He's mine. I call him Satan."

"I'll bet you do," said Pearl. "And who might you be?"

"You can call me Gabriel," said the man. "Miss Maggie figured you'd be coming by, and she thought we could help you."

"Like the angel Gabriel?" Pearl asked.

Behind Gabriel, Miss Maggie let out a peal of laughter. "That ain't likely. Angel. O my Lord." She slapped her knee and cackled. "He's something else all right, but I wouldn't call Gabe no angel."

Gabriel moved aside and let Maggie out on the porch. "This here's one of my regular customers, Gabriel Long. Come on in, Pearl. Luther. I hear you got a price on your heads, so no point standing out in the yard for folks to see."

Over dinner, Miss Maggie said, "Gabe and his gang likes to rob trains, but otherwise they're some great fellows. Brought me my dogs a few years back." Miss Maggie teared up at the thought of her hounds. She nodded. "I figure they could help get your cattle back from that polecat Puckett."

Around the kitchen table were Pearl and Luther along with Gabriel and three other outlaws. Pearl kept staring at Gabriel. She had never seen anyone so dark. Gabriel was the color of night, and probably the tallest, most muscular person she had ever encountered.

Pearl smiled at Gabriel. When he smiled back, his face was transformed into a frightening beauty. She could not help but imagine how Bill Puckett would react to this man.

"I aim to help you two. You saved Miss Maggie's life, and she means the world to me. She's taken care of me through some tough times. She's mighty special," Gabriel said. He looked at Miss Maggie with love. "Miss Maggie's been like a mother to me."

"When can we leave?" Pearl asked. "I want that varmint, Bill Puckett, dangling at the end of a short rope. The sooner he's out of the way the better. He's got my cattle, and I want them back."

Gabriel stood up and motioned to his men. "There's nothing stopping us from heading out now. We can take them, while it's too dark for them to figure out who's got the jump on them."

Pearl leapt to her feet. "Let's go, Third Luther! I want that son of a biscuit eater, and I want him now!"

In his excitement, Luther hopped out of his chair and reached for his guns. He drew them and held them high in the air.

Pearl shouted, "Duck!" just before Luther blew a hole in the ceiling.

Chapter Thirty-four

The colder it got, the closer the cattle bunched together. The range detective's job might not have been cattle ranching, but he did know that sooner or later some of the cattle would be hurt, if he didn't find some respite from the storm. Already, a cow had slipped and fallen on the ice. Leaving his men with the herd, Bill Puckett rode east hoping to find a way out of the basin. He needed a wind break. He remembered a spot along the eastern rim.

Driving winds blew Puckett's horse Pistol sideways, but the mustang held its ground. Trudging onward, the horse pulled against the wind. It was a as though the wind was alive and determined to overthrow Puckett and Pistol. Another gust of wind slammed into the mustang. Against his owner's guidance, the mustang turned back against the gale.

Puckett was furious. He slapped the reins against the horse, but to no avail. Puckett pulled against the reins trying to stop the horse's progress, but to his surprise, Pistol tossed his head and pulled back. The horse stopped. As soon as Puckett let up on the pressure for just a second, Pistol leaped forward, trotting to an overhanging rock along the basin wall.

Puckett had no choice but to let the mustang take the lead. When they reached the side of the basin, Pistol moved along the perimeter to an opening about fifty yards from where they had started. He leapt up the incline and moved away from the basin's edge straight across to a track about a hundred yards long between two mesas. Even though the wind still swept between the rock walls, it was not as forceful. As far as Puckett could see in the fading light, there was plenty of room for the cattle and his hands.

"Hey on, Pistol," Puckett yelled above the wind. "Let's go." Hollering encouragement all the way, Bill Puckett urged Pistol back into the storm and back to the cattle.

At first the cattle did not want to move; they wanted to keep piled together. Soon though, the men had them walking along the edge of the basin. A young cow ran away from the herd into the darkness and the driving wind.

"I'll get her, boss," one of the hard cases yelled.

"Leave her," said Puckett. "I need you more than a damn cow. I don't intend to chase her down."

The hombre looked out into the night. "But boss, she'll freeze to death."

"I said, 'Leave her,'" said Puckett. "Either do as I say or leave. Which is it?"

The outlaw kept quiet and pulled his bandana over his mouth.

Puckett looked smug. "I thought so."

They drove the cattle up the side of the basin and into the valley between the mesas. Sure enough, the wind was not as rough. The cattle soon settled down. One of the outlaws rode to the other end of the valley to take up guard.

Puckett figured Pearl would not come after her cattle at night and in the blowing snow. Still, he did not want to leave himself open to attack from someone else. Too many outlaws knew about the cattle by now. Any one of them might try and relieve Puckett of the herd.

This drove of cattle was headed back to Vernal, back to old man Pecker. Bill Puckett was determined to collect his bounty. Then he had a score to settle with Pearl. He reckoned that Pearl had forgotten that he was the one wearing the britches. He planned to show Pearl how a woman was supposed to act. In his mind, there was only one real way to get the message across. Once he had Pearl under him, she would never go against him again.

Pearl had her own ideas about how a woman was supposed to act, and submitting to any man, especially Bill Puckett was not on her mind. For the moment, her only thoughts were of finding and saving her pa's cattle. She would risk everything to bring those cattle home.

Gabriel found the fallen cow before Pearl did. The cow was lying on her side, her hide stuck fast to the frozen ground. He called one of his men over to help him pull the youngster loose. As the two men struggled to pull her free, the cow bellowed and howled. Pearl heard the commotion and rode up. She leapt from Belle's back and knelt beside the cow.

"Hey, Sugar Booger, it's me. Pearl. We got you, baby. We got you." Pearl wanted to cry. She had raised Sugar Booger from a calf, and she felt like it was her fault that the cow was in trouble.

"Pearl, move out of the way and let us get her up," said Gabriel. "She's going to holler even more when we pull her up. Her hide's going to tear most likely." He grabbed for Pearl's arm to move her out of the way.

Pearl threw her arm out, hitting Gabriel in the chest. "This is my cow. I can do this."

No one noticed Luther digging Pearl's bottle of tonic from her saddlebag. He shook the bottle trying to figure out how much was left. The bottle felt almost full. Luther pushed Pearl and Gabriel aside and knelt beside the cow.

As Pearl struggled to stand, she saw the bottle in Luther's hand. "That ain't a bad idea, Third Luther. After you give Sugar Booger a drink, give me a nip of that."

"I don't rightly see how that's going to help. That tonic ain't nothing but alcohol and getting that cow liquored up is a sure-fire recipe for more trouble," Gabriel said.

Luther looked at Gabriel and Pearl as though they had lost their wits. "Would you move away? It is so dark; I can barely see." He opened the bottle and smelled its contents. The pungent aroma of alcohol filled the air. Luther gagged a little. He ran his hand under the cow to see how tightly she was frozen.

Little by little, he poured the tonic under the cow and tugged against her skin. The cow's skin started to thaw. "This is almost pure alcohol," he explained. "It doesn't freeze, so I can use it to melt the ice holding her to the ground." He poured more of the tonic under the cow.

Pearl and Gabriel eased the cow back, as Luther continued to pull. Finally, he was out of tonic, but by then the cow was almost free. Gabriel grabbed hold of the heifer and yanked her free. Sugar Booger wailed a bit, but Pearl soon had her calmed down. Unfortunately, Pearl was anything but calm.

"That Bill Puckett. When I find his low life skunk-stinking self, I'm going to douse him with water and hold him down while he freezes to the ground. We'll see how he likes being stuck."

Gabriel turned to one of his men. "Take the cow back to Miss Maggie's while we get the rest. I don't want this baby getting away again."

"Okay, boss." The hombre tied a rope around Sugar Booger and led her away.

Pearl and the men mounted their horses, looking for Puckett and the hard cases. They were not anywhere on that end of the basin. The wind was blowing harder than ever. The cattle had to be nearby. There was no way Puckett could have taken them far.

"Let's get out of this hole and skirt around the rim," Pearl hollered over the wind. "They cain't be far."

They rode back up to the opening of the basin. Gabriel and two of his men went one way, while Luther and Pearl rode the other. Pearl looked over at Luther. "Third Luther, I can't thank you enough for what you done. You saved my favorite cow. If'n she'd died, I would've never got over it."

"Let's find Puckett," said Luther. I can almost feel him nearby."

Now Pearl was strongly superstitious. "If'n you think he's here, then he is, Third Luther." She sat straight up in her saddle. Her nerves were totally alert, tuned to the slightest sound. Nothing. Al she could hear was the wind. Then, she heard a muffled cry. A cow was bawling to her right.

Luther heard it, too. "He's there. In that gap. Between those rocks."

They rode for the edge. Suddenly, Luther pulled his horse in front of Belle.

"What in the h-e-double-l are you doing?" Pearl asked.

Luther pointed at a rider hidden by a tree growing out of the rock. The cowboy lit a cigarette. The glow of his match lit up his face for a second. It was one of Chet Miller's kin. Pearl raised her Winchester intending to ventilate the rotten bastard.

"Pearl, wait. If you shoot him, the others will hear the sound." He pulled her beside a pinyon. "Stay here. I'll find our men. Then we can take them all."

Pearl's heart was thudding hard in her chest. "You better hurry up. I ain't got much patience with this bunch."

Luther whirled his horse around and galloped into the night. He almost collided with Gabriel just a few feet away.

"Hold up, Luther." Gabriel grabbed the stallion's reins from Luther. "We got them cornered. I left my men at the other end of the gap."

They rode back to the tree where Pearl was supposed to be waiting. She was not there. Belle was tied to a low hanging branch. Luther pushed against the tree. Then he saw her.

Pearl was crouched under the tree branch where the outlaw was having a smoke. The hombre pushed away from the rock face of the mesa to toss his cigarette away. Without a sound, Pearl jumped onto his back and pulled her knife against his throat.

Chapter Thirty-five

While Pearl was cutting Chet Miller's cousin a neck smile, Puckett decided to settle in and boil some coffee. The wind had almost died down completely, so he built a small fire and started melting a pot of snow. He needed the coffee to warm his innards. He was cold through and though and tired to the bone. Puckett figured he could use a hot cup. Not once did he consider giving his men coffee. Puckett was not the type to share.

Not only was Range Detective Bill Puckett a selfish bastard, he was a cheat as well. Chet Miller's relatives would have fared much better if they had vamoosed the minute they laid eyes on him. He had recognized the oldest of the bunch and planned to kill and collect the bounty on him as soon as he got outside of Vernal. The other men were only wanted on petty crimes. Still, the three of them would be worth about fifty dollars, and he did not have any other use for them.

Puckett counted it lucky that the outlaws were not familiar with his face. He had introduced himself as Bill, and the stupid hardcases had not questioned him any further. Once he had offered them a hundred dollars to drive the herd into Utah, they had not needed any more information from him. They might think him a son of a bitch, but they certainly were not saying so.

The coffee was hot and burned Puckett's throat. He had barely had a chance to taste it, when he heard one of the men come riding into his campsite. It was Jonah, Chet's youngest cousin. He was a dark, curly-haired kid who was meaner than a wet snake.

"Boss, I rode down to holler at Andy back at that end of the valley." He pointed the way he had come. "Thought he might want to take a piss, but he weren't there. Neither was his horse."

"Where do you think he went?" asked Puckett. "Maybe he couldn't wait on you."

"Something ain't right," Jonah said. "He wouldn't have left."

He sounded so convinced that Puckett stood up beside him. "You sure about that, kid?"

"Boss, I've known him since we was kids, and he would still be there. Something's wrong."

Puckett yelled for the men closest to him. Before too long, they had ridden up beside him. "Take the herd to that end of gap. One of you get around in front of it, and you others stay to the rear. I'll find your brother, and then we'll be joining you."

The men wanted to argue, but they were afraid of Puckett. Even so, they took their time turning around and going with the cattle. Once they were out of Puckett's hearing, Jonah said, "You can stay if you want, but I'm getting the hell out of here. Andy wasn't back there nowhere. I looked and looked. All's I found was his cigarette, and it was still burning. I'm telling you something's wrong. It's Injuns or something, but I'm gone."

"I'm with you. I ain't sure that Bill has a hundred dollars. He didn't show it to me," said another of the brothers.

Ignoring Puckett's orders, the three cowardly outlaws rode through the cattle and back out the end of the gap. It was ill-fated for them that Gabriel's men were waiting for them. Bam! Bam! And Bam! The remaining members of the Miller family were deceased. Pearl and Luther went for their guns and headed into the gap, shooting for they were worth. The cattle lit a shuck to the end of the valley, and they would have escaped into the night if not for Gabe's men.

Gabriel Long was a patient man. He rode after Puckett like a tick after a June bug. It was not long, before he was holding Puckett at the end of a gun.

"Don't move, Bill Puckett," Gabriel said. "I believe you hurt a friend of mine. Maggie Fuller's her name."

"I don't know Maggie Fuller, and what's more I don't know you," said Puckett.

Gabriel smiled, but this time it was not a pretty sight. "Well she knows you. I'll make your introduction to her later. Would you like to be living or dead, when she first sees you?"

Pearl and Luther rode up. Seeing Puckett shaking in his boots gave Pearl a case of the giggles. She rode right up beside him and hit him square in the nose. As blood ran down his face, she turned and said to Luther, "Third Luther, I got my cattle back. Let's get a move on."

Without another word, they rounded up the cattle and headed for Miss Maggie's. The wind had simmered down, and the night sky had turned bright and beautiful. Pearl could not remember feeling so happy. Tomorrow, she and the men would start the journey home. She glanced over at Luther. Would he go with them?

Pearl hoped Luther had not changed his mind. For some reason, she knew she needed him. And like her cattle, Pearl would fight to keep him rounded up.

When they reached Miss Maggie's, they bedded down for the night. Luther tied Puckett up in the barn, before they all hit the sack. Unfortunately, Luther could not tie a knot any better than he could shoot a gun, so it was not very long before Bill Puckett had wiggled loose. Puckett retrieved his horse and took off for Vernal. He wanted to make it to Mr. Pecker's ranch before Pearl did. With luck, he could con the old man into paying him anyway.

Pearl climbed the stairs to rest for a bit in the guest room. Before her head could hit the pillow, her eyes closed, and she collapsed. Cattle rustling was hard work, even if she was getting her own herd back. Her last thought was wondering where Third Luther was sleeping and remembering how it felt to fall asleep in his arms.

The next morning after breakfast, Pearl ambled into the barn to fetch Puckett, only to find that he had escaped. Gone. She retrieved the rope Luther had used to tie him up and shook her head. Pearl and the men saddled up and traveled west toward the Uinta Basin. She planned to go about midway along the plateau north of the basin and then head south for the Bench. Most of the folks around Vernal still called the area the Bench. The land around her pa's ranch was open and covered with scrub and cactus. She had lived with lizards and horned toads and battled scorpions, snakes, and mice. With only a handful of women in the Bench, Pearl had been lonely. Women like Rita Lay cropped up more than civilized company, so Pearl had learned to defend herself as well as run the ranch household.

Without Gabriel and his men, she and Luther would have never been able to move the cattle homeward. Now the race was on. Pearl knew if Bill Puckett reached her pa's ranch first, her father would never believe that Pearl has rescued the cattle. In Pearl's experience, Puckett was a two-timing, woman-beating, lying sack of snot. He had murdered Rita's brothers, tortured Miss Maggie and gone after Pearl. She reckoned there was nothing he would stop at to get his way and retrieve a bounty.

Heart racing and blood pumping hard and fast, Pearl drove the cattle homeward as fast as she dared. Even though Third Luther was not much help, he hung in there. His backside had to be as sore as a whore on a horsehide couch, but he never complained. Pearl admired him for that. Gabriel and his men were competent and strong. When Gabriel barked out an order, his men instantly obeyed.

After almost a full day of traveling, Pearl was tired. She and Belle were riding alone, slightly ahead of the herd. The open flatland stretched out before them. To the north were the Uinta Mountains. To the south lay Book Cliff Mountain. Pearl felt free, freer than she had ever felt on the ranch. Pa was never openly cruel to her. He just did not recognize her as an equal—

not in any way. Out here, with the cattle and the men, Pearl felt alive and in charge of her destiny. Part of her dreaded going home. She loved her pa, but she longed for her independence.

Gabriel rode up beside her. Pearl felt his strength emanating from his body. This was a man that had been trapped, but he had broken free to live his own life. She knew that Gabriel did what he wanted to do. He robbed trains, yet he was helping her. Pearl could not judge whether or not Gabriel was right or wrong. She just knew he was strong.

"Pearl, there's someone following us. They're about a half mile behind the herd," Gabriel said.

"Do you think it's Puckett," Pearl said.

"Could be. I won't know for sure until dark. I'll take Luther and double back. We can sneak up on the bastard and catch him."

Pearl laughed. "If'n you want to catch somebody unawares, don't take Third Luther with you. He's liable to shoot your head off. Better to take one of your men. We can handle any varmint what comes up."

"All right, Pearl. Whatever you say. You're the boss," he said. Gabriel pulled his horse around and joined the others, leaving Pearl alone.

"I'm the boss," she said. It felt good. She really was in charge. "I'm the boss."

Chapter Thirty-six

Rita Odena Lay had been jilted. Literally left at the altar by the good-looking dentist—her dream man, Luther Van Buren III. She would have been Rita Odena Van Buren III. Now, she was nothing. It was all Pearl Hawthorne's fault. Her heart burned for Luther, but not nearly as much as her backside. That bitch, Pearl, had not been content with just stealing her man and grabbing back the cattle. No, she had to come along and seduce Luther away from her. Then, Pearl had shot her in the ass end.

Revenge burned hot in Rita's heart. She vowed to get Pearl back. Rita knew just how Pearl would take the cattle back to old man Pecker. Hell, she had used the very same trail to steal the cattle herself. So, she followed behind the herd. Not too closely, because she did not have to.

In the distance, she caught glimpses of Luther. He was as good looking as she had dreamed, but he did not give her the time of day. Rita thought back to the wedding. Luther had not once said she was pretty in her wedding dress. No, hell no! He had taken off like a scalded dog the first chance he got. Maybe, he had cold feet. Rita considered the possibility.

More likely, she figured, he just wasn't the marrying kind. Even though she wanted the high-flautin last name, Rita was not above a little tickle beneath the sheets with the dentist. Her tongue felt the tooth Pearl had tried to knock out. It was tight in its socket. He was a heck of a tooth man, too.

If Rita was going to make her move, tonight would have to be the night. She planned to ease up on the herd after everyone had gone to sleep. The other men with Pearl and Luther looked like outlaws to Rita, and she could not rightly make out the biggest one. He looked dark to her. Rita reckoned he had been out in the sun most of his life. Nothing mattered to her, though, except killing Pearl and taking back her darling dentist.

Pearl might be a vigilante, but Rita had gotten away from both sheriffs and lynch mobs. What was one big-chested bitch to her? Rita was tough, and she considered herself a looker, too. Pearl was no match for Rita Odena Lay.

As the day drew to an end, and the sun splashed her last paintbrush full of color on the western horizon, Rita grew braver. She had nothing to lose and everything to gain by ambushing Pearl. The cattle were kicking up waves of powdery dirt. Rita figured she could take cover in their dust. If she could not see the cowpokes clearly, she thought they couldn't see her either.

On that score she was right, but the flying dirt enabled Gabriel and one of his men to veer north for a way and then double back behind her. As Rita rode closer and closer to Pearl, Gabriel came nearer to her.

As soon as night fell, Rita rode her horse into the midst of the cattle. By now, most of the cows were familiar with her, so none of the animals were spooked. Gabriel hung back to see if she would make a move. Rita watched as Pearl unloaded her cooking utensils from Miller's horse. She waited as the smell of venison and beans filled the air.

Rita had not eaten since the day before, and she decided to eat off Pearl's own plate just as soon as she killed her. The thought of eating Pearl's cooking made her laugh. Rita could not cook worth a damn, so she hoped Luther was not a fussy eater. Her other charms could keep him satisfied. Once they got together, Luther Van Buren III would not be chasing after Pearl Hawthorn. Pearl would be dead, and he would be Rita's forever.

So intent was Rita on her prey that she did not hear Gabriel, until he was almost on top of her. One of the cows closet to her jerked her head sideways. Rita was instantly on her guard. She swung around in the saddle, but it was too late. With a roar, Gabriel flew from his saddle, tackling Rita from hers into the middle of the cattle.

The cattle instantly spread away from the fight. They were bawling and crashing into one another. Pearl and Gabriel's men jumped into the fray, guiding the cattle back into a more manageable bunch. Luther was too astounded to move.

Rita was cussing a blue streak and punching Gabriel. Suddenly, Gabriel pinned Rita to the ground. She wiggled and fought beneath him, until she felt his muscular physique. She ran her fingers up his arm. It felt like a rock, a very hard curvaceous rock. Rita licked her lips. She looked into Gabriel's coal black face. She was instantly attracted to him.

All thoughts of catching Luther and killing Pearl fled from her mind. Only one thought remained—this man. She wanted him something fierce. He felt tough and dangerous. Her arousal communicated itself to Gabriel. When he looked down at the bone-ugly face of Rita Odena Lay, he jumped away.

"Hey sweetie pie," Rita drawled. She held out her hands to Gabriel. "Want to take me...captive?" she looked him up and down. "Tie me up? You sure are big." Her innuendo was clear. To Gabriel, it was scarier than a lynch mob with a new rope.

In a burst of panic, one of the most dangerous train robbers in the West flung himself backward and took off running. Rita jumped to her feet and was hot on his trail. Pearl and Luther and the other hands were struck still as stones. Like lightning on the trunk of a dead pine tree, Gabriel split for Satan, his black stallion, and took off for safer parts.

Rita might have wanted Luther, but that feeling was lukewarm compared to what she felt for the outlaw. She heeled her horse, whipping it and urging it to go faster and faster. Her hair flew into her eyes, blurring her vision. She threw her head back and laughed with wild abandon.

Gabriel's horse Satan galloped as though the hounds of hell were at his heels, and Rita was certainly as determined as a hound dog. She had gotten Gabriel's scent, and she did not intend to let it go, until she had him.

As she rode after him, Rita called out, "Hey, Mister, slow down. I ain't got no grudge against you. Slow down. We can be friends. Good friends!"

Gabriel rode faster.

"Mister, I'm a coming," Rita hollered and heeled her horse even harder.

"Hey, Gabriel," Pearl yelled after him. "Hey, ain't you going to stay and help us?" Pearl could not stop laughing. "I guess he's gone for good." She looked at Gabriel's partners. "You fellows better go and rescue your boss man. Third Luther and I got it from here. We're only a day shy of the ranch."

Chapter Thirty-seven

Pearl and Belle stopped on the knoll overlooking Pecker's ranch. Like the day she had left to find the cattle, snowflakes were whirling in the air. This time, though, things were different. The cattle were right behind her, and so was Third Luther. Pearl felt as though she was on the cusp of a new life. Her heart raced with anticipation, but part of her was also afraid.

A long black cloud flitted across the sky. Pearl caught her breath. It was a bad sign. Then she threw her head back and stared at the cloud, daring it to darken her day. Willing it to dissipate, Pearl gathered her resolve. Without any urging from her mistress, Belle moved forward. Behind them, Luther pushed the cattle into motion.

Suddenly, Pearl let loose, whooping and hollering out, "Pa! Pa! I got 'em, Pa! I got our cattle!"

A scrawny, wind-beaten old man came out onto the porch. He shielded his eyes and watched Pearl and Luther lead the cattle onto his pasture. Nary a smile crossed his face. In fact, he did not seem to recognize his daughter at all.

Pearl did not notice. As excited as a kid with a new toy, she galloped up to the porch, slid from her saddle, and ran to hug her father. She wrapped her arms around his neck and squeezed him in genuine love and joy.

He did not move. He offered no response. Pearl pulled back to look at him.

"Pa, we got the cattle back," she said.

"I see that, girl." The old man's voice was tight. Bitter as gall. "I see you're with that outlaw." He pointed at Luther.

"Pa, he ain't no outlaw. He's a dentist. Rita Odena Lay had him as a mail order fiancé, but he don't want her. I had her captured, too, but she busted loose..." Pearl was talking ninety to nothing, until she realized the old man did not care. He was not listening to her.

"What's wrong, Pa?"

"Hello, Pearl." Range Detective Bill Puckett came onto the porch. "I told your pa everything about you and Mr. Van Buren. I told him about you ambushing me, after I had rescued his cattle."

"Pa?" Pearl reached out to her father.

"Go in the house, girl. I got nothing to say to you."

Pearl as furious. She leapt for Puckett's throat. He knocked her to the porch. She landed on her back at her father's feet.

Jumping from his stallion, Luther drew his Colt and aimed it at Bill Puckett. "You, sir, are a liar. You attacked Pearl and stole the herd, and you know it."

"I know I had a job to do, and this here poster proves it." He held up the wanted poster about Pearl and Luther. "You two attacked a range detective, an officer of the law. Now that I got my bounty, and the cattle are back, I'm willing to go lenient on you. I told Mr. Pecker here that I would release his daughter into his custody and arrest you."

"Pa, it's all a lie," said Pearl. She moved closer to her father. "Pa, what he says is not true."

Old man Pecker slapped Pearl across the face. "I told you to go in the house. You are a shame to me. You revealed yourself. I'll deal with you later." He shoved Pearl in the door and pulled it shut behind her.

Pearl walked into the room like she was seeing it for the first time. It was bare and rough. No pretty curtains, no doilies or pretty rugs. There was nothing for her here. Her chest felt heavy, like it could explode at any moment. All she wanted to do was cry. Cry until she couldn't feel anything else. Ever.

A buzzing filled her ears. She could not wrap her mind around what her father had said. How could Pa believe Puckett and not her? Without thinking, she walked into her bedroom. Nothing had changed. There was nothing *to* change. She realized that. Pa would never see her as an equal. He barely saw her as human. She was just someone to clean up, someone to cook and do all the work. With him, she would never be free.

She reached under her bed and pulled out the bag she had brought from the orphanage. Only two dresses hung on pegs driven into the wall. She folded them and put them in her bag, along with her Bible and a few other articles of clothing.

Pearl heard a shot and fell to her knees. They had shot Third Luther. Either Pa or Puckett had killed an innocent, decent man. All because of her. Gathering the carpetbags to her chest, she started to heave. Sickness, bile, crawled up her throat threatening to suffocate her.

"Pearl."

She heard Luther's voice.

"Let's go. Come on, Pearl!"

Pearl grabbed the bag and ran for the door. Out near the porch, Luther held a gun on Bill Puckett and Pearl's pa.

"Luther?"

"It's up to you, madam. Do you want to stay here, or would you care to depart?"

"I'm departing." Pearl ran for Belle and slung her bag over the saddle horn. "Wait a minute," she called to Luther. She dashed back to Puckett and held out her hand. "My reward, if'n you don't mind. I got them cattle, and I'm taking the reward money."

Puckett hesitated, until he heard the rolling click of Luther's revolver. He handed over the reward to Pearl. "I'll get that money back," he said.

"Pearl, you were told to get in the house. You are being disobedient, girl," said Pecker.

Pearl looked at her father. She felt hollow. Later, his indifference would burn, but at that moment she was empty. "Bye, Pa. Take care of the cattle, cos I ain't no more."

Belle was waiting. Pearl jumped onto her back. Snow whirled faster and faster around them. Pearl did not care.

As they rode away from the ranch, Luther asked, "Pearl, how do I get back to Denver? I think I'm going home."

"Well, I ain't got nothing else to do at the moment, Third Luther. I guess I could ride as far as Denver. Hell, we's both wanted, so it might not be a bad idea to get out of here for a while."

"You're right about that."

Pearl and Luther headed back toward the mountains. Just after they rode into the cliffs, Pearl saw a huge footprint in the snow. It had to be two feet long. Belle stopped and pulled back. The mare would not go any further.

"What is it, Pearl?" Luther asked.

"Shh. I don't know. Something's ahead." She pointed at the footprint.

The print was almost blown away by the snow. Luther laughed. "Your imagination is getting away from you." He rode ahead of her.

Belle danced behind his stallion. Neither Pearl nor Belle wanted to follow Luther into the cliffs. He rode on ahead.

"Luther," Pearl called. He did not answer.

She urged Belle forward, around the rock wall of the cliff. Then she screamed, "Luther, look out!"

Made in the USA
Middletown, DE
07 March 2020